NORMAN MAILER'S LETTERS

ON

An American Dream, 1963-1969

NORMAN MAILER'S LETTERS

ON

An American Dream, 1963-1969

Edited by
J. Michael Lennon

SLIGO PRESS
2004

"Nine Letters from Norman Mailer," excerpted from this
edition, appeared in *Provincetown Arts* 19 (summer 2004).

For
Donna, Stephen, Joseph and James

With a
Special Appreciation
to
The students of English 397, Norman Mailer Seminar, at
Wilkes University

Helene Caprari, Monica Cardenas, Justin D'Angelo,
Patricia Dibble, Katherine Green,
Mark James, Marcia McGann, Sabrina McLaughlin,
Jessica Skutack and Gregory Specter

Contents

Introduction

Until he wrote *An American Dream,* his most evocative and lyrical novel, Norman Mailer did not invest his major fictional characters with his deepest concerns and beliefs: a desire to grow at all costs, a distrust of pure reason, a willingness to take risks, trust in the authority of the senses, faith in courage as the cardinal virtue, fear and loathing for the incipient totalitarianism of American life and, most importantly, a belief in an heroic but limited God locked in struggle with a powerful, wily Devil, conceivably with the fate of the universe in the balance. Stephen Richards Rojack, the novel's protagonist, has these concerns and shares Mailer's theological beliefs. Rojack is a war hero, former congressman, college professor, talk show host, celebrity intellectual and nascent alcoholic. Preternaturally alert to omens and portents and susceptible to every premonition, he hears voices, studies the phases of the moon, and waits for either cancer or madness to strike him. His wife Deborah taunts him with her infidelities and attacks his manhood in a variety of insidious ways, driving him to a physical attack that ends with her murder. Rojack then throws her body out of the apartment window ten stories down to the pavement on the east side of Manhattan. He claims that her fall was suicide, and the brunt of the story is devoted to his attempts to convince his and her friends, the police and Deborah's father, Barney Oswald Kelly, the "solicitor for the devil," of his innocence. Narrated in an edgy, rococo style by Rojack, the novel shows Mailer at the height of his word power as he delineates the dread-filled inner life of his embattled hero. The air of the novel is haunted, swarming with demonic and divine presences, especially in the final chapter, when Rojack confronts Kelly in his penthouse apartment in the Waldorf Towers.

An American Dream was an advance in several ways for Mailer. First, his existential cosmology[1] of a warring universe is fully deployed; second, for the first time in Mailer's work the narrator and the chief protagonist are one; third, all the spiritual dichotomies of the American urban landscape, Mailer's own New York City, are presented. Finally, the novel demonstrated that Mailer had learned how to use his own experience indirectly and creatively. Many commentators[2] on the novel have noted that Rojack has much in common with his creator: both went to Harvard, served in WWII, ran for political office and appeared on talk shows where they discussed existentialism, courage, dread and the primitive. Several noted that Mailer had stabbed his second wife Adele with a penknife (she recovered fully), and that he had undoubtedly and brazenly drawn on this event in depicting Rojack's murder of his wife. While not denying any of these similarities, Mailer responded by saying, "Rojack is still considerably different from me—he's more elegant, more witty, more heroic, his physical strength is considerable, and at the same time he's more corrupt than me. I wanted to create a man who was larger than myself yet somewhat less successful. That way, ideally, his psychic density, if I may use a private phrase, would be equal to mine—and so I could write from within his head with comfort."[3] The novel was controversial from the time it was announced and generated a huge number of sharply divided reviews in literary journals and the mainstream press. It was an immediate best seller[4] and went through several printings in both hard and soft cover. It has been translated into several languages and except for one brief period has never gone out of print.

The story of how the novel came to be written begins in 1963, a very busy year for Mailer. He had a column on religion running every other month in *Commentary* and a column on general topics, "The Big Bite," running monthly in *Esquire*.[5] Two of the columns in *Esquire* grew into major essays, and one of them was the first of several long narratives he was to write about major prizefights. "Ten Thousand Words a Minute" is an account of Sonny Liston's first-round knockout of boxing champion Floyd Patterson on 25 September 1962.[6] Often reprinted and justly celebrated as a masterpiece of the "New Journalism," the essay's success encouraged Mailer and prompted his desire to write about the inevitable rematch of the two heavyweights. During the first half of the year he also assembled his sixth book, *The Presidential Papers,* a collection that was directed rhetorically to President Kennedy.

In January 1963 Mailer split with his third wife, Lady Jean Campbell, the granddaughter of British press magnate, Lord Beaverbrook. She had given birth to his fourth child, Kate, several months earlier. In March of 1963, Mailer met his fourth wife, Beverly Bentley, an actress who was in Hemingway's entourage in Spain during "the dangerous summer" of 1959. Before meeting Mailer she had a relationship in New York with jazz musician Miles Davis. On 31 May, in his emerging role as a public intellectual, he gave a reading at Carnegie Hall that he called "an existential evening," with comment on the FBI, Communism and J.F.K. He made a number of appearances at college campuses in 1963, including one at his alma mater, Harvard. He also published poems, essays, interviews, a futuristic short story and book reviews.

In the summer of 1963 Mailer and Beverly, now living together, took a long automobile trip. First they visited Mailer's army buddy "Fig" Gwaltney in Arkansas and witnessed the ever-memorable autopsy of a cancer victim. From there they drove to Las Vegas where on 22 July they saw Sonny Liston defeat Floyd Patterson for the second time. Mailer had an open-ended arrangement with *Esquire* to write about the fight, which was somewhat less dramatic than the first match. After Las Vegas the couple drove to San Francisco where Mailer spent two weeks on the Beat scene with Don Carpenter, Lawrence Ferlinghetti, Michael McClure and others. A half-dozen times during his rambles alone in the city, Mailer walked narrow ledges, testing his nerve and balance. On the way back, the couple stopped in Georgia for a couple of days to meet Beverly's extended family. She was more than two months pregnant by the time they returned to New York in late August. They were married in Brooklyn in December, shortly after he obtained a quickie Mexican divorce from Jean Campbell. All of these experiences, refracted in subtle ways, would be used in *An American Dream,* which Mailer would begin in September of that year.

In early November *The Presidential Papers* was published, about three weeks before President Kennedy's assassination in Dallas. The collection contained most of his columns, several poems, his September 1962 debate with William F. Buckley, Jr. on the role of the Right Wing, and other assorted prose including his now-celebrated account of the 1960 political conventions, "Superman Comes to the Supermarket," also considered to be one of the foundation stones of the "New Journalism." Although Mailer insisted then and now that he is first and foremost a novelist, the collection contained only one piece of fiction, "Truth and Being; Nothing and Time: A Broken Fragment from a Long Novel." He had been working on this long novel, or "the big novel," as he called it, off and on ever since his Hollywood novel, *The Deer Park* came out in 1955. In 1959 he had raised the stakes by announcing in *Advertisements for Myself,* his first collection of assorted writings, that within ten years he intended to "try to hit the longest ball ever to go up in the hurricane air of our American letters," a novel that "Dostoevski and Marx; Joyce and Freud; Stendhal, Proust and Spengler; Faulkner and even old moldering Hemingway might come to read."[7] In the fall of 1963, however, this big novel was nowhere near completion. Mailer was worried that he might never get back to it, and indeed he never did.

Competing with the desire to get back to the big novel was the desire, or the urgency, he felt to write about the fantastic events, upheavals and people of the period: the Beatles, Castro and the revolution in Cuba, Martin Luther King, Jr., Malcolm X and the civil rights movement, L.B.J. and the escalating war in Vietnam, Barry Goldwater and the Right Wing, "Dr. Strangelove" and American totalitarianism, the second Patterson-Liston fight and a new heavyweight named Cassius Clay, Khrushchev and the Cold War, the astronauts and the space program, the suicides of Ernest Hemingway and Marilyn Monroe and, before and after the assassination, the Kennedys. Another factor was Mailer's need for a regular stream of income to pay for alimony, child support and education, his new apartment in Brooklyn Heights and summer rentals in Provincetown, Massachusetts.[8] Cranking out nonfiction on the current American scene was both exhilarating and a financial necessity. All told, Mailer published 34 separate pieces in 13 different journals and magazines in 1963—the beginning of a periodical blizzard that continued unabated through the decade before slowing in the mid-seventies.[9]

During their stay in Las Vegas Mailer and Beverly went though some emotional somersaults. Their turbulent relationship, and his other experiences on the long cross-country drive, gave him the idea of a short novel focused on the evolving relationship of a man and woman, lovers, driving cross-country to Las Vegas to see the Patterson-Liston rematch. Back in New York in late summer, he began thinking seriously about this short novel and along the way had a brainstorm about how to publish it. In consultation with his long-time lawyer, cousin Cy Rembar, and his new agent, Scott Meredith, Mailer decided to write it first as a serial novel in a magazine in the manner of nineteenth and early twentieth century novelists: Balzac, Zola, Thackeray, Hardy, Melville, Twain, Henry James, Hemingway, Fitzgerald, Andre Gide, John O'Hara and J. P. Marquand. His primary models, however, were Dickens and Dostoevski, who unlike most of the other novelists named above did not complete their serial novels before the first installments appeared. There was no thought of having the entire manuscript in hand in the manner of Henry James. Recognizing his inability to remain sequestered in a long, deliberate effort on a big, Proustian novel while the country was transmogrifying, Mailer decided to put together a deal that would more or less force him to produce a short, dramatic novel in less than a year, and also bring in enough cash to pay his expenses for a couple of more years. Because he already had a column going at *Esquire*, it was the obvious choice for first publication. Sometime after his return from the cross-country trip, Mailer proposed to Harold Hayes, the editor of *Esquire*, that he write a novel in eight installments of 10,000 words apiece that would run in the magazine from January to August 1964.[10] Hayes accepted enthusiastically.

As Mailer explains in the first letter in this collection, he began working on the novel at about the same time in mid-September that he submitted his fourteenth "Big Bite" column to *Esquire* for the December 1963 issue (corroborated by his statement in his 16 October 1963 letter to Eiichi Yaminishi that he had "been working on the novel for the last month"). The *Esquire* containing his column would appear, as usual, two to three weeks before the cover date, in mid-November. The first half is devoted to the 28 August 1963 civil rights march on Washington, but then it shifts abruptly and Mailer announces that this will be his last column in the magazine. After commenting on earlier serial novelists, he concludes:

Well, all proportions kept (please realize that no comparison is intended to Dickens and Dostoevski) there is the desire to try this form. One wants to see if enough craft has been acquired to pull it off. Besides, it appears to be the only way to write the book now in mind without spending two or three years on successive drafts. But one would like to emphasize that there will be no attempt to write a major novel in the next months. The story that is going to appear each successive issue in

10

Esquire will not have the huge proportions and extreme ambition of the big book described in Advertisements for Myself. *No, that work is now to be put aside again. Instead I lay the professional bet in this fashion—I will write eight installments of a novel sufficiently conventional to appear in a magazine. But it will be a good novel. I hope it will be a very good novel. If I fail, the first price to be paid is the large wound to one's professional vanity—if I succeed, well, we may all know more.*

See you next month in the middle of the magazine. One is tempted to call this novel An American Dream.[11]

At the same time that Mailer was selling the serial idea to *Esquire,* Scott Meredith was looking for a publisher for the hard cover version that would follow. Because Mailer still had a contract with Putnam's for "the big novel," and was concerned that the pressure of writing a shorter novel for monthly serialization might affect its quality, he decided to try another publisher. He explained to the *New York Times* that he had felt at the time that *An American Dream* could "be very good, good, bad or very bad indeed, and there would be a lot more pressure on me if I were doing it for a pal [Walter Minton, Putnam's president]. Let a stranger [Richard Baron of Dial Press] take a bath."[12] Consequently, Mailer was released temporarily from his Putnam's contract; Dial got the contract to publish the hardback version of *An American Dream;* and its subsidiary Dell got the paperback contract. As Mailer reveals in the second letter, the hard and soft cover versions would bring him $125,000. Later, the film rights would be sold to Warner Brothers for an additional $200,000, which, when added to the $20,000 he received from *Esquire,* brought the total income received for the novel from 1964 to 1966 to $345,000, a vast sum for any novel in the 1960s. Later editions augmented this total greatly.

Sometime in late summer or early autumn—the exact date is uncertain—Scott Meredith leaked word that Mailer's new novel would focus on the relationship of "a man who takes a 21-year-old girl to La Vegas," as noted in a snippet torn from a *New York Post* column in the Mailer Archive. Even as late as late as mid-October he was still hoping to incorporate an account of the second Patterson-Liston fight in Las Vegas, as revealed in the 16 October letter to Eiichi Yamanishi. Mailer recalled to me that he shifted narrative gears during the course of writing about the hero's murder of his previous wife, Deborah, deciding that this account should be the powerful first chapter of *An American Dream.* The cross-country trip was not entirely discarded, however. Robert F. Lucid, who with Mailer's mother "Fan" first organized Mailer's papers into a working archive, found the manuscript of this narrative on the trip, and describes it as follows:

One fine thing came from examining pages from an unpublished essay Mailer had begun after he and his wife, Beverly Bentley, had

11

*driven out to Las Vegas to cover the second Patterson-Liston fight. The
essay describes a long drive, a stopover with an old Army friend who
was a doctor, and describes further the observing of an autopsy on the
body of a man who had cancer but who went out fast from a burst
appendix. The typescript is reworked in Mailer's hand, changing the
"we" who took the trip to "I"; changing it, that is, to an experience
undergone by Steve Rojack, the hero of* An American Dream. *The
epilogue in the novel as finally published was in fact the beginning of
the novel as composed...[13]*

In addition to using the autopsy in the epilogue, Mailer mined the
long drive in several other ways: Cherry Melanie, Rojack's lover, re-
sembles Beverly in several ways: her blonde, all-American looks, her
spunkiness, her southern background and her love affair with Shago
Martin, who fights with Rojack in chapter seven of the novel. Like Miles
Davis, Martin is a black, avant-garde jazz musician (a singer, not a
trumpeter) with a complex, ironic style whose more adventurous riffs
Rojack describes as "a clash of hysterias." Mailer, in effect, admitted who
his model for Cherry was when he used a photograph of Beverly as part
of the striking dust jacket design he created for the Dial version of the
novel. It seems likely that Mailer picked up some impressions from his
visit with Beverly's family in Georgia that he used in describing Cherry's
southern background. It is certain that the stop in Las Vegas provided
him with material for the epilogue's account of Rojack's four-week stay in
Vegas, "the jeweled city of the horizon" where he wins $24,000 at the dice
tables and calls Cherry in Heaven from a phone booth in the desert.
Mailer and Beverly, after one of their fights, drove out into the desert to
discuss their future now that it was clear that she was pregnant. Finally, Mailer's walks on ledges and edges in San Francisco (which he told
my student, Helene Caprari, were attempts to fathom the emotions and
perceptions of someone considering suicide) enabled him to depict the
perverse "impulse to go out like an airplane in a long glide" felt by Rojack
as he walks around the top of the balcony parapet of Kelly's apartment in
the final chapter of the novel.

Mailer's new conception of the novel came in the wake of his decision
to write about the murder of Deborah—an event originally conceived to
precipitate the cross-country drive. Her full name is Deborah Caughlin
Mangaravidi Kelly. Modeled superficially on Mailer's third wife, Lady
Jean Campbell, Deborah has proven to be one of his most sharply
drawn fictional characters. Her memorability was attested to when he
selected the opening chapter of the novel for inclusion in an anthology
titled *This Is My Best,[14]* as discussed in his 1969 letter to Whit Burnett,
the final one of this edition. Narrative logic required the novel to follow
Rojack though the aftermath of Deborah's murder, though a 32-hour
odyssey of violent threats and confrontations, interrogations, hallucina-
tions, demonic and divine sexual encounters, psychic darts, early

12

morning jazz, epiphanies of despair and a talismanic umbrella used in his half-victory over Barney Kelly. And then the denouement: a long automobile trip, an autopsy, and near-transcendence in a phone booth in Las Vegas. Thus was *An American Dream* conceived and executed.

* * * * * *

The idea for an edition of Mailer's letters on *An American Dream* came during the summer of 2002, which I spent reading the correspondence in the Mailer Archive in preparation for a selected edition of his letters. As I read through those from the mid-1960s, I saw the possibility of a much smaller selection of letters focused on the novel: its creative genesis, sale, writing, serial publication, revision, book publication, popular and critical reception and film adaptation, as well as the many aesthetic, financial and personal considerations surrounding it, as essayed by Mailer in a string of lively letters to family, friends, business associates and admirers. In the spring of 2003 the edition was further developed with the assistance of the ten students in my Norman Mailer seminar at Wilkes University, Wilkes-Barre, Pennsylvania, who helped winnow thousands of letters of the period down to the 76 presented here.

The seminar class also helped me articulate four reasons for this edition: 1) collectively, the letters of this edition cohere into a rough narrative arc that follows the conception and execution of Mailer's plan to write, under deadline pressure, a short opera of a novel in installments for a major magazine, followed by a revised book edition, as well as the reviews and the film version of the novel; 2) the letters were written during an extremely turbulent time in American life, a watershed period that saw, among other events, the assassination of a president and a national black leader, the massive build-up of American troops in Vietnam, and a revolution in Cuba—while Mailer does not comment directly on all of these events, their weight can be felt in the heft of his epistolary style; 3) they provide a rough picture of the busy daily life of a major writer with multiple interests and obligations; we see Mailer *en famille* and share his humor, his financial problems, his marriages and his pride at the birth of his first two sons, his worries about meeting deadlines and his unremitting professionalism; and 4) the letters show Mailer at a culminating moment in his career, the big comeback after the limited successes of all his books after *The Naked and the Dead* in 1948.

Of the twelve major works that followed *Dream* through the 1970s, ten were extremely well received. These ten stand, along with *Naked* and *The Time of Our Time,* his massive 1998 retrospective anthology, as the twelve books of the forty-plus in the Mailer canon that have received the best reviews.[15] The ten are: *Cannibals and Christians* (1966), *Why Are We in Vietnam?* (1967), *The Armies of the Night* (1968), *Miami and the Siege of Chicago* (1968), *Of a Fire on the Moon* (1971),

13

Existential Errands (1972), *St. George and the Godfather* (1972), *The Fight* (1975), *Genius and Lust* (1976) and *The Executioner's Song* (1979). Five of these were nominated for the National Book Award (only *Armies* won), and two (*Armies* and *The Executioner's Song*) won the Pulitzer Prize. This is not to say, of course, that the books after 1979 were lesser works, not when one considers such brilliant creations of Mailer's later years as *Ancient Evenings* (1983), *Harlot's Ghost* (1991), *Oswald's Tale* (1995) and *The Spooky Art* (2003). But however we rate his books—and relying on the scores of reviewers is a dubious method at best—the fifteen years from *An American Dream* to *The Executioner's Song*, from 1965 to 1979, are arguably the most sustained period of achievement in Mailer's continuing career.

Note: Except for standardizing the format, Mailer's letters are reproduced here exactly the way they looked when signed, with the following exceptions: a small number of typos and/or spelling errors have been silently corrected, and a few obviously dropped words have been added in brackets. Nothing from the originals has been omitted, as Mr. Mailer requested.

Endnotes

1. Mailer's first extended explanation, in 1958, of his belief in an embattled God is still the best. See "Hip, Hell, and the Navigator: An Interview with Norman Mailer." By Richard G. Stern and Robert F. Lucid. *Western Review* 23 (winter 1959), 101-9. Reprinted in *Advertisements for Myself* (Putnam's 1959); and *Conversations with Norman Mailer*, edited by J. Michael Lennon (University Press of Mississippi 1988). See also Laura Adams's interview, "Existential Aesthetics: An Interview with Norman Mailer," *Partisan Review* 42, No. 2 (1975), 197-214, also collected in *Conversations with Norman Mailer*. For an extended discussion of Mailer's theological beliefs, see Lennon's "Mailer's Cosmology" in *Critical Essays on Norman Mailer* (G.K. Hall 1986).

2. The most important essays on *An American Dream*, as well as the most important reviews and interviews, are listed in Appendix II.

3. Mailer, quoted in an interview with an unidentified interviewer, "Norman Mailer on *An American Dream*," *New York* Post, 25 March 1965, 38; reprinted in *Conversations with Norman Mailer*. The other significant contemporaneous interview on the novel is Nancy Weber's, "Norman Mailer's 'American Dream': Superman Returns," *Books (New York Post)*, March 1965, 14-16.

4. The novel rose to number eight on the *New York Times* bestseller list on 11 April 1965.

5. "The Big Bite" commenced in *Esquire* in the November 1962 issue and ran through December 1963. "Responses and Reactions," a series of columns devoted mainly to discussions of Martin Buber's *Tales of the Hasidim*, ran every other month from December 1962 to October 1963.

6. "Ten Thousand Words a Minute" was the February 1963 "Big Bite" column in *Esquire*. Mailer's title encapsulates two facts: the length of the column—approximately 20,000 words—and the number of minutes Floyd Patterson was on his feet before being knocked out in the first round by Sonny Liston: 2:06.

7. *Advertisements for Myself,* 477.

8. In "Mr. Mailer Interviews Himself," he states: "I did *An American Dream* in installments because I was in debt and had to make a small fortune in a hurry. That didn't make it a bad book. I think it's my best book. I confess I still believe sentence for sentence *An American* Dream is one of the better books in the language." *New York Times Book Review,* 17 December 1967, 40. Reprinted in *Conversations with Norman Mailer.* See Appendix IV to see where Mailer added and subtracted words.

9. A complete, annotated list of Mailer's publications year by year, 1941-1998, can be found in *Norman Mailer: Works and Days,* by J. Michael and Donna Pedro Lennon (Sligo Press 2000). Appendix I lists Mailer's key publications, 1948-2003.

10. The richest account of the circumstances surrounding the publication of the novel in *Esquire* is Carol Polsgrove's *It Wasn't Pretty, But Didn't We Have Fun: "Esquire" in the Sixties* (W.W. Norton 1995). See also Hilary Mills, *Mailer: A Biography* (Empire Books 1982); and Peter Manso, *Mailer: His Life and Times* (Simon and Schuster 1985). Appendix III provides a timeline of some of the key events in Mailer's life and the life of the nation from 1962 to 1966.

11. "The Big Bite," *Esquire*, December 1963, 26. Never reprinted.

12. Mailer, quoted in Lewis Nichols's column, "In and Out of Books," *New York Times Book Review,* 14 March 1965, 8.

13. Robert F. Lucid, Introduction to *Norman Mailer: A Comprehensive Bibliography* by Laura Adams (Scarecrow Press 1974), xiv-xv.

14. Whit Burnett, editor, *This Is My Best: In The Third Quarter of the Century* (Doubleday 1970). Mailer's letter and the selection from chapter one of the novel are on pages 99-110 of Burnett's collection.

15. Over 400 reviews in 25 major periodicals of 27 of Mailer's books from 1948-1998 are rated in *Norman Mailer: Works and Days.*

16. Mailer, quoted in Herbert Mitgang's article, "On the Scholarly Trail of the New Revisionists," *New York Times,* 10 February 1983, C-22.

Acknowledgements and Appreciations

My first debt is to Norman Mailer, who gave full access to his Archive and generously supported the preparation of this edition. He has also read his letters collected here, provided countless details for the head notes and introduction, and corrected many errors of fact and interpretation. I am deeply grateful for his help and friendship. The ten students of my English 397 Norman Mailer seminar at Wilkes University made major contributions. During the spring 2003 semester they helped select the letters and gave extra time on weekends for this work. In addition, members of the seminar key stroked the manuscript, proofread the result and did supplementary research on the historical period, the novel's background and reception and Mailer's correspondents. Seminar members also compared the two versions of the novel in various ways, which was of great help in evaluating the changes Mailer made when he revised it for book publication. They also helped me (especially Marcia McGann) organize and re-file the letters from the mid-sixties in a systematic way. The seminar also provided great encouragement and engaged me in regular dialogue about the problems, large and small, encountered in preparing this edition. I am happy to express my gratitude to Helene Caprari, Monica Cardenas, Justin D'Angelo, Patricia Dibble, Katherine Green, Mark James, Marcia McGann, Sabrina McLaughlin, Jessica Skutack and Gregory Specter. Jacqueline Mosher, Humanities Division secretary at Wilkes, also deserves applause for her above-and-beyond support.

About twenty years ago Hershel Parker compared the two versions of the novel and published his conclusions in *Flawed Texts and Verbal Icons* (Northwestern University Press 1983). His essay, and a copy of his working papers donated to the Archive, was quite useful and stimulated important discussions in class. While I do not agree with Parker that the *Esquire* version is the better, there would seem to be some substance to his general argument that subsequent authorial or editorial changes to the first published version of a text may significantly damage its creative integrity. Mailer was also impressed with Parker's painstaking comparison, but told the *New York Times,* "I think the Dial version is the better. The publisher preferred to print the *Esquire* serial, but I devoted four months to revising it for the book."[16]

Several colleagues and friends read drafts of the text, making invaluable contributions. First among these is Robert F. Lucid, Mailer's authorized biographer, whose familiarity with the materials surrounding the novel and rich knowledge of Mailer's life helped me at every turn. His assertion of the importance of Mailer's summer 1963 cross-country drive to Las Vegas was of particular value. Barbara Wasserman provided regular encouragement and a great deal of background information on the Mailer family and the events of the early 1960s; she also proofread the manuscript with an eagle eye. Darin Fields, my Dean at Wilkes University, gave me strong encouragement and advice at the outset and, as then-chair of the Humanities Division, approved the Mailer seminar where much of the work was accomplished. Thomas Fiske, Mailer collector and enthusiast, also read the manuscript, noting errors and providing encouragement, as did Jack Scovil, former colleague of Scott Meredith. Monica Cardenas and Sabrina McLaughlin made many useful suggestions when they proofread the manuscript (and regularly discussed the shape of this edition with me); Mark James did a thorough analysis of the *Esquire* and Dial versions, including a final word count of each chapter. Mailer scholar Barry H. Leeds has generously read the final manuscript and made several thoughtful suggestions. Stephen Borkowski, Provincetown neighbor, has been of great assistance on this project, generating advance subscription sales, reading the manuscript, listening, cheering and advising from start to finish. He also introduced me to Peter Madden who graciously assisted in locating a binder for the edition. Peter Lennon has supported my work on Mailer for decades, providing good advice and many obscure documents. Joseph Lennon did a careful review of the introduction and was an inspiration to me as I compiled the index. Christopher Busa, Publisher of *Provincetown Arts*, has also been a stalwart advisor and source of encouragement. His magazine will publish nine letters from this edition in the magazine's annual issue, published in July 2004. Finally, Professor Harold E. Cox of Wilkes University has freely given his time and counsel on complex production problems. To all those, named and unnamed, who have assisted, my thanks. The errors that remain are solely my responsibility.

The Eugene S. Farley Library at Wilkes University provided support for this project during the spring semester of 2003 when the Mailer seminar met in the Norman Mailer Room on the Library's first floor. Thanks to Brian Sacolic and Heidi Selecky for arranging for this support. I would also like to thank the Faculty Development Committee of Wilkes University for providing a summer 2002 research grant, which enabled me to undertake preliminary work on the project in Provincetown, Massachusetts, Mr. Mailer's permanent home since the mid-1980s. The Faculty Development Committee and Wilkes University also supported my participation in the April 2003 American Literature Association Conference in Cambridge, Massachusetts where I delivered a paper on the letters published here. I would also like to acknowledge the encouragement of Jay Parini, the editor of the recently published *Oxford Encyclopedia of American Literature*. I have borrowed a few paragraphs from my literary biography of Mailer in volume three of this massive reference work and reworked them for this introduction.

Finally I would like to thank my wife, Donna Pedro Lennon, for her unstinting help and encouragement on matters technological, editorial, and psychological. Her support has been crucial. No one has done more to make this volume a reality.

The Letters: 1963-1969

TO: AMBASSADOR GUTIERRES-OLIVOS

Mailer's letter to Gutierres-Olivos, the Chilean ambassador to the United States, is the first to acknowledge his plan to write An American Dream. *He began the novel shortly after writing the letter.*

142 Columbia Heights
Brooklyn 1, New York
September 18, 1963

Dear Senor Gutierres-Olivos,

I want to thank you for your invitation to take part in the round table on October 10, but I fear I must say no because I expect to be away in New England at that time, working on a novel.

Yours sincerely,
Norman Mailer

TO: ANDRE DEUTSCH

Mailer's letter to Andre Deutsch is the first to lay out the plan of serial publication of a novel in Esquire *followed by hard cover publication by Dial Press and soft cover publication by Dell Books. Deutsch (1918-2000) was the principal director of Andre Deutsch Limited, Mailer's British publisher from 1959-1966. Mailer married Beverly Bentley (1930-), his fourth wife, in December 1963. Alain Robbe-Grillet (1922-) is a French novelist known for the flat, objective descriptions of his novels. The "big book" Mailer refers to is the one he promised in* Advertisements for Myself *(1959), a novel "fired to its fuse by the rumor that once I pointed to the farthest fence and said that within ten years I would try to hit the longest ball ever to go up into the accelerated hurricane air of our American letters." Walter Minton was the president of Putnam's, Mailer's American publisher of four of his books from 1955-1967, but not, as the letter indicates,* An American Dream, *which was still unnamed at that time. Charles "Cy" Rembar (1915-2000) was Mailer's first cousin, longtime lawyer and sometime literary agent, although it was Mailer's new agent, Scott Meredith (1923-1993), who helped broker the deal with Dial and Dell after Mailer himself had successfully proposed the idea to Harold Hayes (1926-1989), the editor of* Esquire. *Corgi, an imprint of Transworld Publishers Limited, published the soft cover British edition of* Advertisements for Myself *in 1963. Diana Athill (1917-) was an editor and director at Andre Deutsch.*

142 Columbia Heights
Brooklyn 1, New York
October 15, 1963

Dear Andre,

First, a long belated thank you for the cook books, which Beverly [Bentley] received with glee and from which I expect to draw dividends over the years. They are, by the way, damn good books. I read parts of a few of them just for pleasure. They stack up very nicely against [Alain] Robbe-Grillet.

Much has happened since I saw you and doubtless you've had wind of it. I came to the grim conclusion over the summer that I was just not going to be able to do the big book well, considering my financial situation, because although the advance royalties were quite decent I still would have been able to work only two weeks a month on the novel and the other two weeks would have to be given over to getting my pen hired for the best going price, or else giving lectures for fees. These secondary activities are always chancy and they open the danger of using up more effort than is commensurate. So I decided the only way out of my impasse was to dare a bold stroke. I contracted to do a novel in eight installments for *Esquire*, talked Walter [Minton] into releasing me for one book, and managed to sell this absolutely unwritten work for an incredible sum to Dial and Dell. This is in the strictest confidence, but they are paying me $125,000 against the hard cover and paperback rights and so of course this solves my difficulties for a year or two, or ideally three or four. Now all I have to do is write a first-rate novel in eight months, and I can tell you this gives me pause. At any rate, I won't be working on the big novel for about a year (I think I'll need four months to recuperate from the next eight months) and that was why I told Cy [Rembar] to tell you that I didn't wish to draw royalty payments yet.

Now as far as this new book goes, I'm quite ready to work up a contract with you right now if you so desire, but I think it might make more sense to wait and see how the book turns out. If it's a good book I might ask you for a fairly good royalty for it. If it's a bad one, I obviously could not. But if we wait there at least would be no feeling of A) holding you up or B) giving something away. And you can have my word and my hand across the sea on it that I will certainly give you first and complete crack at the book. In any case I don't feel there's a vast rush on this—at least I'm in no hurry. So if you'd like to wait and see what you're buying, that will be fine with me. Incidentally, to the best of my understanding all this happened very quickly, the paperback rights have already been bought by a subsidiary of Dell who paid a vast price—twenty-five grand, my friend, again in the strictest confidence. What bothers me about this last is that I've been very pleased with Corgi for the job they have been doing, but the English paperback rights were tied into this deal and I had reluctantly to go along with it, since Dial and Dell were paying so much for the American rights. I'm going to write a letter to Corgi today so they won't bounce too hard when they get the bad news.

And when I see you this January—I certainly hope you'll be making a trip this year—I'll tell you the story of how the ante got up so high. It's a rare account of the mating habits of that most curious bird—the American publisher.

Say hello to Diana [Athill] and my best to you,

Norman

TO: ALAN EARNEY

Earney was an editor at Transworld Publishers Limited, which under the Corgi imprint published the British soft cover edition of Advertisements for Myself *in 1963. Victor Weybright was an editor at Andre Deutsch.*

> 142 Columbia Heights
> Brooklyn 1, New York
> October 15, 1963

Dear Alan,

I was quite pleased with the cover of *Advertisements* that you put out. You really do good jackets over at Corgi, and if *Advertisements* doesn't do well, the physical production of the book can hardly be blamed.

But now I have a bit of news which I expect will prove upsetting to you. Caught in a financial situation which seemed to offer no issue, I talked Walter Minton into releasing me for one novel, and I'm now going to do a serial which will be printed in ten-thousand-word installments over the next eight months. I also signed a contract with Dial and Dell for hard cover and paperback rights and they agreed to pay a vast, indeed an unbelievable sum for the book. As part of the arrangements they insisted upon buying the English paperback rights for a paperback company which is their subsidiary or associate in England. I did my best to try to strike this last clause, because as I say I've been quite pleased with the way you've presented my books. In fact, as I all but told Victor Weybright, you were doing a tastier job. But the amount of money was so vast and indeed the amount offered by the English paperback company was so great, that I was not able to afford to refuse this extra specification of the English rights. Indeed there was not even opportunity to consult you, for the transaction took place in a record forty-eight hours. The wheeling and dealing was much like Hollywood. While I know this news can give you small pleasure, I would like to repeat that I have no ill feeling towards your house—quite the contrary—and expect that we'll be together again after this serial is published.

> Cordially,
> Norman Mailer

TO: REED WHITTEMORE

The poet Reed Whittemore (1919-) was editor of Carleton Miscellany.

142 Columbia Heights
Brooklyn 1, New York
October 15, 1963

Dear Reed Whittemore,
   Ah, thank you for you invitation, but it can't be done. I'm in trouble.
I'm writing a novel for *Esquire* over the next eight months and since
this by definition is a serial, I am suffering the perils of Pauline. Could
you send me a copy of the symposium when it comes out?

Best, etc.,
Norman Mailer

TO: EIICHI YAMINISHI

*Mailer never met Eiichi Yaminishi, his longtime Japanese translator.
The book referred to in the first paragraph is* The Presidential Papers,
*which was published on 8 November 1963. It contains his account of the
first heavyweight boxing match between Floyd Patterson (1935-) and
Sonny Liston (1932-1970) on 25 September 1962, titled "Ten Thousand
Words a Minute," first published in* Esquire *in February 1963. Mailer
did not incorporate an account of the second fight into* An American
Dream *(the "short novel"), but the fact that he was considering doing so
shows how open-ended his plan was at this point. He did, however, use
portions of an essay tracing his cross-country trip with Beverly Bentley
in the summer of 1963, including his stop in Las Vegas for the fight, in
the novel's epilogue. Mailer submitted each installment two months
before* Esquire's *publication date (two weeks earlier than the month on
the cover), except for the last three, all of which were late. The final
installment was about ten days late.*

142 Columbia Heights
Brooklyn 1, New York
October 16, 1963

Dear Eiichi,
   This is just a quick note, for as always I have much too much mail to
answer. There should be copies of the book in another two weeks, and
I've left instructions at Putnam's that they are to send out one of the
very first copies they receive from the printer to you. If I'd realized it
was going to take this long I would have sent you the galleys, but
believe me, Eiichi, the book was not attractive in galleys and I preferred
for you to wait until you saw the finished version.

As for a note on the second Patterson-Liston fight, I fear that I cannot satisfy you in this because if I started to say one word I would end with close to a hundred thousand words. In fact, I'm thinking of incorporating the second fight into a short novel (80,000 words) that I'm going to write in serial by installments of 10,000 words a month for *Esquire*. I've been working on this novel for the last month and have just finished the first installment. As soon as there are galleys, I'll send them to you. This is most definitely not the big novel, but I hope it will be a good one. Perhaps it will be interesting for some large Japanese magazine to publish the installments month by month. I took on the book because I was in need of money to finance the larger book, and by one of those curiosities of American publishing, I ended up receiving a fantastic advance royalty. I'm almost ashamed to tell you what a capitalist this makes me, but they will pay $125,000 for the hard cover and paperback rights in America. I mention the size of this figure because it may help you to get a greater price from any Japanese magazine interested in publishing it, and that of course would be of benefit to us both. I would like just once that you make some money as well, for the arduous work of translating.

This is dictated in a great rush, for the burden of writing ten thousand good finished words a month in a novel to which I cannot return takes up so much time that I cannot afford the leisure for time now of a quiet correspondence. So please, as ever, accept my warmest good wishes for you and your family.

Norman

P.S. That figure I named is of course not being paid by *Esquire*, but by the publisher, Dial Press, and by the paperback company, Dell. If you wish a note added to "Ten Thousand Words A Minute," perhaps it might be a good idea to insert it yourself, just saying that I'm working on a novel which may include the second Patterson-Liston fight.

P.P.S. I never took the opportunity to thank you for the list you provided me, but it was most entertaining and interesting to read, and I sent a copy to my publisher.

TO: WILLIE MORRIS

Mailer met Morris (1934-1999) in New York after Morris became editor of Harper's *in 1963. Mailer's letter gives a hint of the lifelong tension in his writing life between his profound desire to write novels and the financial need to write shorter pieces of nonfiction. He resolved the problem, to some extent, in the late 1960s and early 1970s, by writing long nonfiction narratives that are fictive; they read like novels. Three of these,* The Armies of the Night *(1968),* Miami and the Siege of Chicago *(1968) and* The Prisoner of Sex *(1971) appeared first in* Harper's. *All three were nominated for the National Book Award;* Armies *won it and a Pulitzer Prize as well.*

142 Columbia Heights
Brooklyn 1, New York
October 21, 1963

Dear Willie,

Let me thank you for your letter, but writing articles has a bit of drudgery to it for me, and now I'm free, for a year at least, to work on a novel, so I think I'll be keeping myself much to myself through this long winter. I'm glad you're at *Harper's* and let me wish you good luck in what you're doing.

Best,
Norman Mailer

TO: ANDRE DEUTSCH

The explanation of the relationship of Scott Meredith, Cy Rembar and Mailer provided in this letter is a response to the anxiety Deutsch conveyed in a 24 October letter about Meredith's methods and Mailer's two weeks of silence. Barbary Shore *(1951) was Mailer's second novel. The parenthetical reference to the title of the* Esquire *novel is one of the first in a letter. He mentions it again in the next letter to Alan Earney. Mailer met Jeanne Johnson when he was in Bellevue; he was sent there for psychiatric observation after stabbing his second wife, Adele Morales (1925-), with a penknife on 20 November 1960. He introduced Johnson to Paul Krassner, editor of* The Realist.

142 Columbia Heights
Brooklyn 1, New York
November 4, 1963

Dear Andre,

This is just a note to say that we must not have any trouble or misunderstanding between us. Scott Meredith is a top money agent, and can get advances like nobody else I've ever known in the literary world, but some of his methods I suppose can seem fairly strong-arm if one is on the receiving end, so I'm writing this to tell you that all final decisions on everything are still being made by Cy [Rembar] and me. As you may remember my telling you once in Cy's office just before we got together again, I had a bad conscience toward you about *Barbary Shore* and have no desire to get into that again. So look, Andre, and straight: I wish as a working rule of procedure that you will assume things are going well between us unless you hear directly to the contrary from Cy or me. If our silences are sometimes long, it is because

24

the variety of work one is engaged in creates the delay. The last letter I wrote to you must have been in my mind for a month, but I was desperately at work on the first installment and did not want to take the chance of breaking a writing day by starting it with a letter. By the time I was done for the day I usually felt too drained to dictate something coherent. The delay which took on, under the circumstances, a large significance to you really had none for me.

As for the advances you've paid already on the long novel, what do you want to do about them? Would you like them returned? Or should they be applied to whatever arrangement we've made for *The Presidential Papers,* or what? Any course is agreeable to me except one. I do not want to be owing you this sum for the next year or two.

A friend of mine named Jean Levy—she is married to Julian Levy, a Surrealist gallery owner—wants to do a Moroccan cookbook. She's got a Moroccan woman working for her who must have been one of the finest Moroccan cooks in America—I can certify this, having been their weekend guest. So naturally I told her of your extraordinary list, and promised that I would write to you and ask if you're interested in such a venture. Jean used to work in advertising and I'm certain can write well enough to do a good introduction. And present the recipes in an agreeable fashion.

I'm writing to Corgi today to tell them that of course they're welcome to do the Dial-Dell book (now titled *An American Dream*) if they can outbid Mayflower.

Glad Diana's book is doing so well. I look forward to receiving it.

Two copies of *The Presidential Papers* should be on their way to you this week.

I don't know what's up with Mrs. Timson, since I've been out of touch with all those people for quite a while. A telegram might get her to reply.

Jeanne [Johnson] (my ward) is now Mrs. Paul Krassner, 318 East 18th Street, New York City. I finally got around to buying her a wedding present: two marmosets, with which we're all pleased.

Everything else is fine.

Best to everyone,
Norman

TO: ALAN EARNEY

The public was informed of the novel's title in Mailer's final "Big Bite" column in Esquire, December 1963, *which was on newsstands in mid-November before the assassination of President Kennedy. Mailer had written the column much earlier, of course, turning it in to the magazine in mid-September.*

142 Columbia Heights
Brooklyn 1, New York
November 4, 1963

Dear Alan,

Apparently the situation is not so final as I thought when writing to you last. I was under the impression that Mayflower had bought the rights to *An American Dream* (which is the title of the novel under discussion) but it seems that they merely have an option to give a first bid and match any counter bid, so I don't know that we're necessarily closed off from one another altogether. Anyway, let's see how the book turns out. In the meantime,

my best to you
Norman Mailer

TO: ADELINE LUBELL NAIMAN

A college friend of Mailer's sister Barbara, Lubell (1927-) met Mailer in 1946. In 1947, as an editor at Little, Brown, Naiman argued unsuccessfully against Bernard DeVoto for the acceptance of The Naked and the Dead, *published a year later by Rinehart. Mailer married his third wife, Lady Jean Campbell (1930-) in April 1962; they were divorced in December 1963. Lucky is Adeline's husband, Mark Naiman. Jean Malaquais (1908-1998) was one of Mailer's closest friends and his intellectual mentor. They met in Paris in 1947. The "last piece" in* The Presidential Papers *referred to in the penultimate paragraph is "The Metaphysics of the Belly," a long, philosophical self-interview about art, digestion, disease, Hemingway, Picasso, technology and the soul. Mailer liked it enough to reprint it in* Cannibals and Christians *(1966), along with a new, companion self-interview, "The Political Economy of Time."*

142 Columbia Heights
Brooklyn 1, New York
November 5, 1963

Dear Lub,

Your letter came just as I finished dictating a long series of letters this morning. It was a pleasure to read, almost as if I'd been given a

26

reward for working so hard at so dull a task through the morning. I'm in a curious situation now which makes me accumulate my mail for a month or more, then answer it in a day. I've always done this, but now it takes on the sterner forms of discipline, because I'm engaged in a break-neck venture. I got into trouble financially and was in debt, and decided the only way out of it which would give me some kind of modest luxury—like spending $20 on a dinner for two without thinking about it, or buying theatre tickets when I felt like it—was to write a novel in serial for *Esquire*, eight installments of ten thousand words each, and then sold the book before a word was written to Dial and Dell for $125,000 bucks. It seems that I am finally hot again as a property. For this next year I'm in the soup because this novel's got to be fairly good or I'll be ambushed by more crossfire than anybody I can think of in recent years, and indeed will deserve to get the worst, so I am off and writing. I've finished the first installment which is sheer cliff-hanger, and the second installment, which is sheer cliff-hanger. Can I keep it up?

Also my personal life has taken quite a turn. I've been living with a blonde actress named Beverly Bentley since last March, and she is now pregnant, which we desired, and we'll be married if and when I get a divorce from Jean. For Campbell is being cute and difficult about it all. I won't tell you anything more about Beverly for I'd rather you meet her and decide for yourself. I have a feeling you may like her.

When I last heard from you, the baddies had Lucky over a barrel. What has happened since? You make no mention of that in your letter. Give me the details if you have the chance. I'm curious.

Finally I have a new book. It's called *The Presidential Papers*, and will be out in about ten days, and I'll send you a copy this week—just so soon as I get some from the publisher. There's only one important piece of writing in it, the last piece, which I think is pretty good. As for the rest, if you're bored and want some top-flight intellectual action, why don't you look up [Jean] Malaquais, who's now living in Wellesley. His address is 1 Horton House, Washington Street.

And forgive the flatness of this letter. It doesn't mean I have no feeling for you, it just means I'm bored to death with writing letters. The trouble is I still enjoy receiving them.

Love,
Norman

TO: FRANCIS IRBY GWALTNEY

Mailer served in the Army with "Fig" (1921-1981), a teacher, novelist and native of Arkansas. During a visit there in March 1975, he introduced Mailer to the woman who became his sixth wife, Barbara Norris Church Mailer (1949-).

142 Columbia Heights
Brooklyn 1, New York
November 9, 1963

Dear Fig,

I really enjoyed the hell out of your last letter and have taken a month and a half to get around to answering it only because I've gotten caught up in a job of work which could be killing if it gets going wrong. I decided the only way out of my financial hole was to take a jump, and so I contracted with *Esquire* to write a novel in eight parts, each installment (ten thousand words) will appear in a successive month, and since I didn't have anything behind me when I started, it comes down to writing a book in eight months, which has a finished draft good enough to make it a good novel. I did, however, succeed in selling it to Dial and Dell before I started for a price so large it's crazy, and what's good about this is that I'll have economic freedom for a couple of years and may be able to do my big book in relative calm.

Incidentally, the agent I had who brought this deal off was a real live wire who accomplished a hell of a lot for me—his name is Scott Meredith—and so if you're dissatisfied with John when the time comes to get a new book published, maybe it would be worth your while to let Scott take a crack at it.

Things are going along quietly in New York with lots of work, and Bev and I take off for two weeks each month to the country, either to Provincetown or to Jamaica, Vermont, and there I sweat the fat drop and try to do my work. I'd love to get out to Ruston to see you this winter, but I don't think there's too much chance of it, what with the work schedule. Maybe if I get fed up with the East I'll go out to do my two-week's stint in Louisiana. But the trouble is that I'm very poor company when I'm writing and so hesitate to visit friends at such a time. If the impulse ever did take me, what airplane route does one take to get into the vicinity of northern Louisiana?

This letter isn't as long as I'd like it to be, but that's because I haven't answered any mail in a month and so as usual I have to knock off sixty letters in a day and half.

Give my love to your sly-boots lady and to Yee-Yee and to Frank. Bev sends her love,

Norman

TO: EIICHI YAMINISHI

Henderson was a Japanese translator who worked on the poems in The Presidential Papers. *Josh Greenfield, a friend, visited Japan regularly.*

Dear Eiichi,

First I want to thank you for all the trouble you took in analyzing the separate connotations of each word in the haiku. The error on *miezu* is not Henderson's fault, but mine. I don't know how it happened, but it is inexcusable for I'm usually most careful about such matters. My guess is that the error cropped up in the galleys and I did not check them carefully enough. At any rate, I hope you will correct it in *The Presidential Papers* or add a note about the error. Incidentally, Henderson's literal translation of the poem gives soon for *vagate, indication* for *keshiki,* and *appear-not* for *miezu.* His translations are often very free, but since he is scrupulous to give a literal translation first of each word in the haiku, one is free to make one's own translation. In this case I use Henderson's version. Truthfully I did not think I could improve upon it, for it is one of his best. I agree with you that *cry* is much too open as a sound and does not give the sensuous equivalent of a locust's chirp, but the difficulty is that we have no equivalent in English for the double sound of the locust's voice, nothing like *koe,* and so a sound like *chirp* is too closed. One could substitute something like *tick-tock went the locust,* which might give more of the feel, but tick-tock has unfortunate connotations for it is used often in children's nursery rhymes, and *cry,* while unfaithful to *Basho,* is a most evocative word in English. If ever I have the fortune to come to Japan and the opportunity to study the language for some months, I think that I might try to begin by immersing myself in the haiku for I have a suspicion that the secrets of the Japanese language may be contained in the form. Certainly I have the impression that one of the great differences between Japanese and English is that English is constructed upon the narrative line of the voice, in which the natural break in association is the pause to take a breath—whereas Japanese may be built more upon the interval between each blink of the eye. So many of the haiku gave me the impression of a short but exquisite movie.

A week or two ago a letter came from Josh Greenfield, in which he spoke warmly, even dithyrambically about you, and said in passing that my reputation is very high in Japan. I know, dear friend, that this is due more than anything else to the devoted, sensitive and intelligent work you have done on my behalf over all these years. I'm only too aware of that, but someday I hope I will have the opportunity to shake your hand and talk to you across a table. It was a fortunate day which brought your first letter to me.

Now for the news of the serial. I've completed the first two installments and should have galleys of the first to send to you within a week. It's fairly good so far but of course there are many difficulties and ambushes ahead. If I can keep the level up to the first two installments

29

I think I will have however a novel we need not be ashamed of. The difficulty of course is the lack of time. An average of ten to fifteen thousand words a month is not too bad in itself, but the fact that one must do this every month does increase the strain. I would describe the novel to you but I have a natural reluctance for summary and indeed would prefer you to pick up the first installment with no sense at all of what is to come. So if you will be patient for a week I think your announcement will gain force from the fresh impact of the first installment on you. For the present, it may be enough to say that it will be a short novel (90 thousand words) in the nineteenth century tradition, to wit, it is concerned with good and evil, and its exploration will take the form of a narrative with a reasonably developed plot.

As for the rest, I would like you to use the picture which is on the back of the jacket of *The Presidential Papers* for that book. I do not know which picture Josh Greenfield refers to but the photograph in the rocking chair catches the mood I was in when I was writing the introductions for the collection.

In any case, my dear friend, I await your reaction to the first installment of the novel. It is, by the way, to be called *An American Dream,* and the first installment has the chapter title of "The Harbors of the Moon."

My warmest regards to your wife and to your children,

Norman

TO: EDMUND SKELLINGS

Skellings (1932-), then a professor at the University of Alaska, Fairbanks, and an admirer of Mailer's work, met Mailer at an Esquire *symposium at the University of Iowa in December 1958. He saw Mailer again when Mailer visited Alaska in early April 1965; Mailer drew on his impressions of the visit for his 1967 novel,* Why Are We In Vietnam? *Mailer turned in the third installment shortly after the first one appeared in* Esquire *in mid-December.*

142 Columbia Heights
Brooklyn 1, New York
November 26, 1963

Dear Ed,

This is just a note because I have to start tomorrow on the third installment of the novel I'm doing in serial for *Esquire* so I'm trying to drive the bulldozer through my mail.

I can't answer your questions the way they should be answered—I did however send your manuscript to Walter Minton yesterday, who's my publisher at G.P. Putnam's Sons, and told him that you were interested in rewriting it. So let's see what happens there.

Best for now,

Norman Mailer

TO: DAVID SUSSKIND

Mailer appeared on "Open End," a television talk show hosted by David Susskind (1920-1987), in early November. He debated William F. Buckley, Jr. in Chicago on 22 September 1962 on "The Role of the Right Wing." The debate transcript was published first in Playboy *(February 1963) and later in* The Presidential Papers. *Mailer sometimes drafts his letters in pencil, sometimes dictates them, and sometimes uses a tape recorder. His secretary at the time, Anne Barry, took dictation and then typed the letters for his signature as she found time. The time lag between dictation and typing explains his lack of comment on President Kennedy's assassination four days earlier, both in this letter and the two preceding.*

142 Columbia Heights

Brooklyn 1, New York

November 26, 1963

Dear David,

Thanks for your letter. I must confess that I thought the show was pretty bad while we were doing it, and for the first time in my life I really felt for you, since none of us were doing very much on our own. To my surprise, the reactions I got were more favorable than almost any show I've been on. How odd is audience reaction. Actually, David, if you'd like to invite me back, there's one show and one show only I'd really like to do right now. And that is a mano a mano with Bill Buckley, just you, me, and Old Bill. I think I could take him over two hours, and take him good, but win lose or draw it could be an exciting show. There is interest in the two of us as opponents. Our debate in Chicago for instance was a sell out in Medinah Temple, and grossed $8000.

If you are interested in this, we'll have to pick the time most carefully, because I'm deep in work this winter and doing a novel in serial in *Esquire*, and my deadlines fall each month between the 9th and the 15th. Which means that the only time I can afford to take off a few days and get ready would be in the week after I hand in a particular installment.

At any rate, best for now,

Norman

31

TO: MARY JANE SHOULTZ

Mary Jane and Ray Shoultz were acquaintances. Mailer's letter to her confirms the fact that Esquire *usually appeared approximately two weeks before its cover date. It also demonstrates his eagerness for feedback on the opening installment.*

> 142 Columbia Heights
> Brooklyn 1, New York
> December 11, 1963

Dear Mary Jane,

I'm buried in mail today so this is just a line to ask you to let me know what you think of the first installment of the serial, which should be out about the time you get this letter. That is, if you have the time in your own busy life.

How is Ray? I take it he's completely recovered. I certainly hope so.

Don't worry about the delay at Random House and *Esquire*. Those places take forever.

> Best for now,
> Norman

TO: EIICHI YAMINISHI

Tuttle was an employee of a Japanese publishing firm that published Mailer's works. The "paragraph" Mailer refers to is a 175-word tribute to Kennedy, part of a symposium in the 26 December 1963 New York Review of Books *titled "The Fate of the Union: Kennedy and After." Mailer revamped it for the "Special Preface" to the Bantam soft cover edition of* The Presidential Papers *that appeared in May 1964.*

> 142 Columbia Heights
> Brooklyn 1, New York
> December 15, 1963

Dear Eiichi,

Just a quick note to answer your questions in your letter of December 9. The man who arranged *The Presidential Papers* and the new novel, *An American Dream*, is an agent named Scott Meredith, and the annoyance with Tuttle occurred only because in the general pressure of other work I forgot to recognize that this would affect your situation in Japan. It is all and entirely my fault. I should have had the wit to remember when I gave them the foreign rights that this could cause you embarrassment. I'm afraid I can offer no excuses. I have a bad head for business and this complication slipped my mind entirely. However, on Monday I'm going to call them up and get this straightened out, and in fact I'll delay mailing this letter until after I've spoken to them. So look for a continuation to this in the P.S. at the end of this letter.

As for Kennedy, I've been very depressed, too depressed to write more than a paragraph which I've already sent to you. It was, incidentally, printed in *The New York Review of Books,* which is the one good review in America and has issues appear every two weeks. And in fact, it will be sent to you, for I took out a subscription for you. At any rate, I have no desire to write more now because the event is not only deeply depressing but enormous in its ramifications. Kennedy had personal charm—one misses him certainly that way—he was also nothing exceptional as a politician, rather a conventional middle-of-the-road leader of the Democratic Party. What was lost is an intangible good. There was a particular magic or let us say liberty surrounding Kennedy which enabled one to be critical of him in a way that had been impossible in America since the War, and all sorts of subtle but exciting changes were occurring in America's culture. In Marxist terms, while Kennedy did nothing to shift the nature of productive relations, he opened the way, *whether he wished to or not,* for dramatic, even radical, changes in the superstructure. To use myself personally as an example, my function shifted in these few years from some sort of mysterious half-notorious leader of the Beat Generation, a sort of psychic guerilla leader, in fact, to something quite other, a respected if somewhat feared leader of the literary Establishment. And that change was terribly important, because in America one can accomplish very little change from outside the Establishment, whereas inside one's words can even have a curious influence upon the leaders. And I fear that that, possibly for a good many of us, is now smashed altogether.

My best for now,
Norman

December 16
P.S. Just now I spoke to Henry Morisson of Scott Meredith Literary Agency, Inc., (580 Fifth Avenue, New York 36, N.Y.; cable address: Scottmere), and told him that you were to have complete and final say-so on all Japanese matters, and that he would please instruct Tuttle to that effect. Morrison promised to send a telegram today to Tuttle clarifying the matter and passing on my instructions that in all matters Tuttle is to obtain your final approval. This gives you complete power over Tuttle, Eiichi, and I think it would be best to have as little to do with Tuttle as possible, because I have found that when I have the power to make decisions but continue to work with other people that I tend to give away some of my power in embarrassment, forcing myself to accept suggestions I don't really like in order to save the feelings of the other person. At any rate, what happens next is up to you, but I would prefer that you go on making arrangements for me by yourself as you have in the past. I think the most Tuttle would be useful for is to give us some idea of the market and of what can be gotten for a novel.

Norm

TO: MICKEY KNOX

Knox (1921-), one of Mailer's closest friends, met Mailer in Hollywood in the summer of 1949, which Knox recalls in his memoir The Good, The Bad and The Dolce Vita *(2004). In the late 1960s, Knox acted in the dramatic version of Mailer's 1955 novel,* The Deer Park *and two of Mailer's experimental films. Mailer met the poet Richard Wilbur (1921-) in Paris in 1948. The book he refers to in the third paragraph is* The Presidential Papers, *the dust jacket of which depicted Mailer sitting in a Kennedy-style rocking chair. The "movie piece" in the fourth paragraph refers to Mailer's desire to sell the screen rights to the novel to Hollywood, which he eventually did. Joan was Mickey's third wife and the sister of Mailer's second wife, Adele Morales (1925-). Mailer's friend Roger Donoghue was a professional boxer in the 1950s and early 1960s. Mailer introduced him to his wife Faye Mowery in Provincetown.*

142 Columbia Heights
Brooklyn 1, New York
December 17, 1963

Dear Mick,

The Kennedy thing hit very hard here. Women were crying in the streets (mainly good-looking women), a lot of middle-aged Negroes looked sad and very worried, and then we all sat around in gloom and watched the television set for the next seventy-two hours. Altogether it was one of three events having something profoundly in common: Pearl Harbor Day and the death of Roosevelt being the other two. And the Ruby-Oswald stuff was just too much on top of it. I haven't felt like writing a word about the whole thing, I've been too fucking depressed every which way. The main loss I think was a cultural one. Whether he wanted to or not Kennedy was giving a great boost to the arts, not because Jackie Kennedy was inviting Richard Wilbur to the White House, but somehow the lid was off, and now I fear it's going to be clamped on tight again.

As for Oswald and Ruby, I don't know what was going on, but I don't have the confidence we'll ever know. I'd like to believe that the FBI had a sinister hand in all of this, but somehow I doubt it. I suspect the real story is that two lonely guys, all by themselves, put more grit in the gears than anyone ever succeeded in doing before, and it's just a mess, a dull miserable mess.

The book of course falls by the side in all of this, one of the million minor casualties. With Kennedy alive it was a good book, but with him dead, it's just a curiosity, and somehow irritating in tone. I don't even mind the loss of it in a funny way.

As for the movie piece, there's been a startling lack of interest in it, and no nibbles at all. I think if someone had five or ten million bucks, it could make a great movie. But I suspect it's not going to be bought until something else I write is made into a movie and makes a lot of money. The trouble with it is that it's not the sort of thing that can be done by an independent producer on a small budget because to be successful it would need epic treatment.

Which somehow brings up your remark about "intellectual adventurer." I'd forgotten that you said it, but your mention of the fact brought it back to me, except that you mention it in an altogether different way, using the phrase approvingly. The character around Kennedy who said it was of course using the term spitefully.

As for the debt, I guess you're right. I had of course not forgotten the cruel repayment I exacted by giving you that C.K. research project. Somehow I had the impression there was another debt. I realize now, thinking about it, that I'm dead wrong. So accept my apologies, old buddy. When you're back, we can exchange wedding presents. Incidentally, I saw Joan one night at the fights. She went with Roger and Faye [Donoghue] and I held up the other end because Beverly was tired that evening. We were sort of friendly but a bit cool, and she was kind of sweet, got tired early, and went home early. She said something about going back to Europe sooner than she originally thought she would. Who knows, she might even be missing you. As for the wedding itself, Roger was not excluding you. The only people present were Bev and me (because I was the best man) and a girl named Fifi Bergman who was bridesmaid for Faye. At the last moment Faye's best friend and her boyfriend arrived from Pittsburgh, but it isn't as if fifteen or twenty people arrived and you were passed by. That's the truth, Mick. Roger's really fond of you. I've never heard him say a really bad word about you. You're right that Roger doesn't have too much sympathy with my ideas, but then, what the hell, Roger was still taking his pitch from the Journal-American when I met him, and while I've had some influence on him I expect I'd be surprised if I had had a really large influence because we started from preconceptions which are too far apart.

The scene here is quiet. Much hard work for me and then more hard work. I'm plugging away on the serial and now have gotten through the third installment. It's a pretty good book so far but I just hope and pray I can keep it up, because the strain is tremendous. It's like being an old pro and fighting an eight-round fight when you're not in the best of shape. Anyway, if I can bring it off, next year ought to be more relaxed.

I'm damn sorry you left when you did. It always takes us a couple of weeks to loosen up around each other and this time was a damn shame because I think we're really getting to the point in our lives where our respective ears are getting better and we can listen more carefully to what each other has to say. The passing glimpses you've given of Yugoslavia are fascinating and if you get a chance, let me hear a little more of your impressions.

Love,
Norm

*Stendhal (1788-1842), Marcel Proust (1871-1922) and James Joyce
(1882-1941) are writers much admired by Mailer.*

142 Columbia Heights
Brooklyn 1, New York
December 20, 1963

Dear Fig,

Now you've really got me curious to read the rejected novel. Is your
only copy at Secker and Warburg? Or could I get a chance to see it? I
don't want to moralize, but the difficult thing about writing well when
one is angry is that the truth of it tunes up one's whole body physically
so you tend to lose the cool sense of each moment passing into each new
moment in your book. That sense of knowing when you're right and
when you're getting off your balance. I know when I'm mad, I tend to
accelerate not only in the physical speed with which my hand writes
down the words but I also telescope the progression of the ideas and so
something which makes sense internally to me is hysterical in its
external manifestations. If it weren't for this difficulty I think anger
might be the best single emotion to write out of, for it firms ups one's
balls and burns out all the half-shitty half-loyalties to people who we
don't really like or admire.

I'm working sixty days ahead of publication (that's my automatic
deadline); I've now finished the first three installments of the serial.
Everything is fine so far except that I can't describe a screw as thor-
oughly as I might like to, and I ain't moving quite as fast as I should be
moving. In the first three parts I don't think I've gone a quarter of the
way. It's a little like giving a course and taking too long on the earlier
writers so you find you have one lecture left for [Marie-Henri Beyle]
Stendhal, and a half lecture for [Marcel] Proust, a half lecture for
[James] Joyce. But writing the serial is in itself fun. It makes me
work. Since it's been eight years since I've set out to write a novel and
finish it, I think I would have taken forever to get somewhere if it
weren't for the fact that I have to make my decisions in great haste and
stick by them. It's a little like playing ten-second chess. You have to
take the bold choice each time, because you know you can depend on
getting something out of the bold effects—the subtler choices may prove
too subtle and fail to come to life in the speed with which you have to
write. I don't know how good the book will be, but it's interesting
writing a serial. I'm not so sure I'll say when I'm done, I swear, never
again. Since I, like you, used to be very much of a second, third, or even
fourth draft novelist, it occurs to me that much of the possibility in this
may have developed over the last twelve months when I was writing
against a deadline once or twice a month and so formed the habit, for
better or worse, of having my first drafts become the basic body on

which the final result was clothed.

Anyway, that much for shop. Bev is coming along nicely and should have the baby by the middle of March. She hasn't put on any weight since this summer except around the middle, and we're both looking pretty good, although I am definitely on the plump side. If I get any fatter I'll need an old skinny gal like Ecey to shake some life into me. But now you tell me Ecey's getting plump too. God almighty.

As for *The Presidential Papers,* I'll send you off a copy tomorrow. I was working so hard on the serial that I goofed on preparing a list of friends to get the book, and so practically no one I know has received a copy. Only my enemies. The publicity girl at Putnam blithely went ahead and sent out copies to people I don't even speak to. That's the literary life, dear friend. Incidentally, you'll find the book very odd reading. Like everybody else, I discovered I cared a lot more about Kennedy than I thought I did, and so his death was directly depressing, and turned much of what I wrote. A lot of it seems off balance now. Anyway, let me know what you think.

And love to Ecey, Yee Yee, and Frank, Jr.

Merry Christmas
Norm

TO: RITA HALLE KLEEMAN

Kleeman was a staff member at P.E.N., the international writers organization. Mailer served as President of the American branch, 1984-86. His letter turning down her invitation to speak is similar to many others not included in this edition. The gregarious Mailer knew that he had to say no or fail to complete his installments on time. The speech at Wesleyan University was a notable exception.

142 Columbia Heights
Brooklyn 1, New York
December 20, 1963

Dear Rita Halle Kleeman,

Normally I'd say yes and be pleased to be part of your discussion on March 2, but I'm afraid it's not possible to speak anywhere for the next six months, since I'm doing a novel in serial form for *Esquire* and it takes up just about all of my time. I spoke at Wesleyan last week, and was not able to prepare properly, and had cause for embarrassment in the result. Now I'm also stuck for a debate with William Buckley after the first of the year, but outside of that nothing this year, nothing. Maybe 1965.

Yours sincerely,
Norman Mailer

TO: DON CARPENTER

Carpenter (1931-1995) was a west coast novelist who corresponded regularly with Mailer in the 1960s. Michael McClure (1932-), Beat poet, musician and playwright, was a major figure in the San Francisco Renaissance of the 1950s and 1960s. Mailer wrote a preface to his play, The Beard (1967). Mailer saw them in San Francisco during the summer of 1963.

142 Columbia Heights
Brooklyn 1, New York
January 15, 1964

Dear Don,

My letters are getting as short as short hairs. The serial has me close to pissing blood because the ten thousand more or less finished words each month screws me tight as a twisted wire. So when I finish, as I've just done with the fourth installment—I have to stay two installments ahead to meet the magazine's schedule of deadlines—I usually fall on the mail like a demented zoo animal and do my best to eat it up. So this is really just to say that I liked your letter of December 22 which you sent December 30 and the praise was fine, and I just hope I don't let everybody down. Because a good beginning is one thing, but "the keeping up" (which is Henry James' little language for it, of course) is something else. Anyway, at this point, the trip is still being taken alone. Let's see if there's snow blindness near or far out on our fields. And let me hear what you think of the second installment if you're in the mood. Despite my remarks about the praise up above, you are, buddy, believe it or not, free to register disappointment. For one thing each installment is sixty days behind me so I'm worried more about where I am now than where I was then, and also if something is not good enough one's friends are only hurting one's sense of reality if they neglect to tell you.

Say hello to Mike McClure if you see him and give him my best. Tell him I'd like to talk to him about his *Meat Science Essays* if we get a chance.

Best,
Norman

TO: VANCE BOURJAILY

The novelist Vance Bourjaily (1924-) met Mailer in New York in 1951 and introduced him to several writers. Theodor Reik (1888-1976), the American psychologist, was an early and brilliant acolyte of Sigmund Freud (1856-1939).

142 Columbia Heights
Brooklyn 1, New York
January 16, 1964

Dear Vance,

The serial business is excellent for straightening out one's life, since there's no time to do anything but work. Years ago, Theodor Reik was being analyzed by [Sigmund] Freud, and as a talented young man he was naturally interested not only in being a superb analyst but a musician, a writer, a lover, a boulevardier, a vigilante, even a mad genius. Freud listened and got angrier and angrier. Finally he said, "Reik, you want to be a big man? Piss in one spot." So that is what the serial business puts you up to.

Actually, it's like ten-second chess. You have to make your decisions in a hurry and depend on the probability that the professionalism you've acquired over the years is backing you up, that the bets are good and solid and that you're enough of a gambler to take an occasional long shot which excites you. I think one benefit from writing a serial is that one could give a good practical course in how to write a novel afterward, for you spend most of your time dealing with the simple mechanical aspects of book writing. Never before has it been quite so important to get a character out of a room with a minimum of sweat.

I feel for you as a hunting guide. Not to mention us amateurs who land on your door. There will be all the bad pros who arrive with a drink in their eye and the remark, "Vance, baby, I feel like I got to kill something this year." The worst thing about writing a book is the afters—all the obligation one has to be loyal to its logic. So you have to put up with guys like me who invite themselves to go hunting with you. I feel half bad about this. I sure as hell want to come out next year for a few days; you sure as hell may wish to do some work or to go hunting by yourself. So can we leave it that I accept your invitation with pleasure but that it is understood that you are free to change your mind if later on the thought of my arriving gives you, for a hundred good reasons, no particular sense of the agreeableness of things. And I in my turn expecting that your excellent manners will overcome your excellent instinct asking you this, should I buy a shotgun? What would be a good shotgun to buy? I know nothing about them, and so half like the idea of handling one for some months before I get to fire it.

Give my best to Tina, and hear ye, I'm married again, and to the young lady you met last spring, Carnegie Hall evening.

Best,
Norman

TO: EIICHI YAMANISHI

142 Columbia Heights
Brooklyn 1, New York
January 17, 1964

Dear Eiichi,

Just a quick note. I finished the fourth installment, and so once again I'm rushing to get through my mail. The first installment was sent out to you last week, and the galleys of the next two installments mailed out a day or so ago, so you should have the first 32,000 words by the time you receive this letter. The only thing I would suggest is that you state what you think is necessary in the clearest and simplest terms to Henry Morrison, because while he is a very able agent it's possible that he does not know too much about the situation in Japan, and I think in such cases it is a mistake to make him aware of all the complexities. He is likely to start worrying and playing a larger part himself. You see, I'm afraid that if he plays the main role, he will start consulting Tuttle again, and it is my impression that whenever Tuttle appears on the scene, people start trying to pry certain rights away from you. So if you want to write the negotiations for me in Japan, that's fine, Eiichi; if you would rather have someone else take up such a work and merely consult you for advice, then let me know that, too. Whichever course you desire is completely agreeable to me, my dear friend, but I was not certain from your last letter which course you prefer. Just tell me exactly what you wish and I will arrange it with Morrison.

As for the rest, I hope to take a week's vacation and go skiing, and then in a few days I have a debate on television with William Buckley. It is however not live, but taped.

My very best to you, Eiichi, and to your fine family,

Norman

TO: HARVEY BREIT

Mailer became friendly with Harvey Breit (1909-1968), a reporter and novelist who spent summers on Cape Cod. Breit profiled him in the New York Times *in June 1951.*

142 Columbia Heights
Brooklyn 1, New York
February 11, 1964

Dear Harvey,

Just a note. I've been down in the mines working on my novel, five installments now done, three to go—mortal terror all around that I will run out of gas. I must say, each installment gets worse than the one before. Then when I finish, there's a snow bank of letters around, all the mail that's accumulated during the month. So I send this off to you in the ill humor of being written out, smoked out, hung over, and in a bitch of a mood about the novel. But I write to you anyway because I wanted to say hello and tell you that we miss you and hope you'll be back soon.

Outside of work everything's going along fairly well and New York seems quiet. I hope Mrs. Lowry's agreeable.

Salud,
Norman

TO: MICKEY KNOX

Nothing came of the idea of having Orson Welles (1915-84) play Henderson and Sonny Liston play Dahfu in a film version of Saul Bellow's Henderson the Rain King *(1959). Knox attempted unsuccessfully to convince Orson Welles to buy the rights.*

142 Columbia Heights
Brooklyn 1, New York
February 17, 1964

Dear Mickey,

This is the worst day in the world to write you a letter because I'm in a foul mood and have forty other letters to get through before the day is done. But if I don't write you today another month will go by, because what with the serial taking up almost all the time, I try to take care of all the mail once a month. Anyway, there's very little in the form of news. I'm simply working my ass off, and going out very little, seeing very few people, and keeping my nose over the top of a pencil. In return, things have been quiet and nice here. Bev's pregnancy has been going along pleasantly and my life has been for me remarkably stable. Sometimes a week goes by before I get a chance to do some serious drinking. So that's it on the news.

The biggest excitement in New York this year culturally has been "Dr. Strangelove" and the arrival of the Beatles, who, surprise, sounded kind of nice when I saw them on television. And "Dr. Strangelove" you've got to see. It's the only great movie I know which is great not because it's great as a movie but because it's sociologically great that the thing was made.

I hope things are going ok between you and Joan. How's her pregnancy? I'm a little pissed off at her because I asked her to ring and say goodbye before she left and she didn't, which bugs me somehow. I mean like, you know, I knew her when.

41

I feel apologetic about this letter because your last one was fascinating and full of news, and this one of mine reads like last week's newspapers, but truthfully it's not depression, it's just the weight of work. I was thinking about you yesterday and the couple of good evenings we had just before you left, and I wished you were back in New York again.

Best, Mickey, and love,
Norm

P.S. I think *Henderson the Rain King* could make a great movie, so here's wishing you luck on that. I'm sure you've thought of this, but it occurs to me that [Orson] Welles might be interested in playing Henderson; and it might be interesting to try to get Sonny Liston to play Dahfu. If you can get a picture started, I'll go and talk to Liston because I'm on fairly good terms with his manager, Jack Nilon.

TO: CHARLES H. SCHULTZ

Schultz was an official with the New York chapter of the National Academy of Television Arts and Sciences who invited Mailer to take part in a forum discussion.

142 Columbia Heights
Brooklyn 1, New York
February 17, 1964

Dear Mr. Schultz,

Normally I think I would want to say yes to your invitation for the Forum, but since it falls on March 12, which is three days after I'll be handing in my next installment [the sixth] of my novel to *Esquire*, I can know to a certainty that it will be impossible to prepare anything for the Forum or even think constructively in advance about what I would like to say and what my ideas might really be. So for that reason, most regretfully, I'm afraid I must decline.

Yours sincerely,
Norman Mailer

TO: EIICHI YAMINISHI

142 Columbia Heights
Brooklyn 1, New York
February 19, 1964

Dear Eiichi,

Again just a note. I've just finished the fifth installment and now must go through all the mail of the last month, so there's not time to write properly to anyone.

I made an arrangement for you to get tear sheets (that is to say, pages cut from the magazine before it appears each month) when they are ready. Thus in another three weeks you should get the fourth installment and in seven weeks, the fifth installment, which I've just finished. In other words you will be receiving each installment of the novel seven to eight weeks after I've finished it. If you think this is too slow and you would rather have galleys, we can shorten the time to about four weeks, or indeed if speed is altogether essential I can make arrangements to have a typewritten copy of each installment sent to you a week or ten days after I finish it. However, this last may be hard on your eyesight, for the first typewritten copies which are easier to read have to go of necessity to the hard-cover publisher and the paperback publisher here, and as you know, a third or fourth carbon is no joy to work with. At any rate, dear Eiichi, let me know what is most comfortable for you.

As for a copy of previous novel contracts of my novels, let Anne Barry know if you've not received them, and she will get in touch with Mr. Rembar and ask him to send it to you.

I was pleased you liked the first three installments so much. The fourth and fifth gave me great difficulty but I think that they have not, so to speak, "lost" the book. I still have the chance to make this a good novel and as I approach the last three installments the problem becomes exciting, almost as if one were in a race.

Outside of that, no news. Isn't it true that when one is working hard there is never any news, just work. Please say hello to your children and to your dear wife, and ask Toshio and Michio to accept my best wishes for their entrance examinations.

Warmly,
Norman

P.S. Your letter of February 10 just arrived and I was wondering if it is worth the difficulty to have the book appear in serial especially if they plan to print it in five installments rather than in eight, because the novel is being constructed on the form of eight separate chapters. Again I leave it to you to do whatever you consider most wise, but I thought it would make it easier for you to play your hand if you know that I have no particular insistence it be printed as a serial in Japan.

TO: VAHAN GREGORY

The deadline for the sixth installment passed a week before Mailer wrote to Gregory, a literary acquaintance.

142 Columbia Heights
Brooklyn 1, New York
March 16, 1964

43

Dear Vahan,

Just a note to thank you for your very good and fine letter. I'm up to my nose in the serial—since I have to keep two installments ahead of *Esquire*, I'm banging away now in the pits of the sixth installment, trying to avoid a let-down, and reminding myself I've only two to go, so forgive the brevity of this.

Best,
Norman

TO: GEORGE LEA

George Lea was a writer friend.

142 Columbia Heights
Brooklyn 1, New York
March 17, 1964

Dear George,

Thanks for your letter. It was practically inspirational, old buck. Actually, I feel very far from being a citizen of the world these days. There's something about trying to do a novel in eight months which overcomes all the outposts of one's ego, so that you recoil back on the thing you can do reasonably well, which is to be some kind of half-ass professional. So I don't feel important these days, I just feel wrung out, worn down, near to written out, scared, like a semi-final fighter at the end of six rounds with two big ones to go. You know what I mean.

If you get a chance, drop me a line about the novel you're working on, and what it's about.

Best for now,
Norman

TO: MARTIN PERETZ

Now editor-in-chief of The New Republic, *Peretz (1939-) was a professor at Harvard when Mailer met him in the early 1960s. Mailer watched Cassius Clay, later known as Muhammad Ali (1942-), defeat Sonny Liston for the heavyweight championship in Miami on 25 February 1964.*

142 Columbia Heights
Brooklyn 1, New York
March 17, 1964

Dear Marty,

Thanks for your letter. I'm not sure I'm going to go into a ski cabin next year, for it proved expensive, and full of headaches this season.

I still have my nose deep in the serial and I'm not sure I ever want to write a novel this way again. For cumulative fatigue may get in the way of finishing the book properly. I hope not, I think I still haven't lost the book, but I'm feeling wrung out, dull, and smoking too many cigarettes these days. Forgive the lugubrious tone—I think I'm still recovering from the Clay-Liston fight. One of my secret dreams was to see Patterson and Liston have a great third fight.

Best for now,
Norman

TO: ANDRE DEUTSCH

Mailer had almost caught up by the seventh installment, which was turned in only a few days late.

142 Columbia Heights
Brooklyn 1, New York
April 16, 1964

Dear Andre,

Up to my armpits in the serial—installment seven is getting done. Only one more to go. The trouble is it will have to be about twenty thousand words long. So this is just to say that the agreement we made with Leonard Russell is all right with me. Hope to have a full book to show you soon.

Best to Diana,
Norman

TO: LOUIS and MOOS MAILER

The late Louis Mailer was the brother of Mailer's father, Isaac Barnett "Barney" Mailer (1891-1972). He and his wife Moos lived in South Africa but visited the U.S. several times. Beverly gave birth to Michael Burks Mailer, Mailer's first son, on 17 March 1964. Mailer had obtained an extra week to write the final installment, which would be twice the length of each of the first seven.

142 Columbia Heights
Brooklyn 1, New York
April 17, 1964

Dear Louis and Moos,

Just a quick note to tell you a little about Michael. The work on the serial is really reaching up to its climax now, and I'm in a dozen kinds of trouble, for I have to finish the book in the next five weeks and the

45

last installment has fearful importance attached to it because the book can turn out anywhere from fairly good to very good by the way I end it. At any rate, in the midst of all this, Mikey B. was born, and an alert little devil he is, very sharp-eyed and lively he is, like a squirrel, with a head that now is very much like mine in shape—nothing to brag about, but since he was born with a cranium as long and thin as a banana, we consider this a blessed improvement. In any event he looks more like his mother than like me. He's got her eyes and nose, her lower lip and chin. Which are, in turn, almond-shaped, uptipped, tremulous, and pointed. But his ears and upper lip belong to me, the ears quite large, but disposed benevolently close to the head. The upper lip is pure Mailer. Thin, as bowed as Cupid's bow, and the channel in his upper lip is deep and long. He eats all the time, is passing fond of his mother, and glares at me. I'm obviously the opposition. And I suspect he's planning (with the aid of his four sisters) to pull off a palace coup in the next ten years. As for the rest, he's got a barrel chest, very active somewhat skinny legs, quick-moving arms, quiet red-gold hair (not much), and a fabulous twig, which persists, despite all odds, at remaining in a state of constant erection. It must be all the women he's surrounded with. Last, he looks to be a good boxer. The other day I tapped him with three left hooks, and before I could land a fourth, he brought up his right to cover his chin. Add to this that he has a low but nonetheless noble brow, a fifty-year-old air of British elegance and looks disconcertingly at times like Dwight D. Eisenhower or Winston Churchill. (At other times he just goes back to looking like a squirrel.) His toes? Oh god, I haven't looked at them yet.

Love to you, my dears, and I'll send pictures so soon as we get a good one, which will probably not be until the summer.

Norman

TO: MICKEY KNOX

Adele Morales Mailer (1925-) is the mother of Mailer's second and third children, Danielle "Dandy" (1957-) and Elizabeth Anne "Betsy" (1959-).

142 Columbia Heights
Brooklyn 1, New York
April 19, 1964

Dear Mickey,

Yes, you did win a bet, and in fact everyone in town has come around to remind me that I owe them money. I must have made twenty bets it would be a girl. Mike is 30 days old now and very alert. He moves like a boxer. I threw three left hooks to his cheek and on the fourth he brought up his right to block it. Karate I leave to you. He kicks like a

Georgia mule. He's got my head and will probably have my forehead, Bev's eyes and nose, his upper lip is like mine, and the lower lip and chin belong to the mother. It's weird watching him make a face because some of his expressions are identical to Bev's. She claims many of his expressions are like mine, but of course I'd be the last to see that.

I've got something funny to tell you about the birth. When I spoke to Adele about it I told her that Beverly had four tough hours at the peak of labor, but a good strong delivery, and was feeling fine. When Adele saw Beverly she said, "Norman tells me you had a dreadful time." If there's anything worse than a woman, it's an ex-wife.

Incidentally, Adele says she's planning to visit you and Joan for a month or two this summer. If it isn't that big a drag, try to convince Adele (that's a joke, son) to stay on in Europe an extra month and go around traveling. Get her fired up on seeing something or other. The reason is that I would like to have Dandy and Betsy for two months this summer instead of one, and probably won't be able to if Adele comes flying back like a scared rabbit. I know that's no easy matter to accomplish, but see what you can do. If you can get Joan to think it's her idea, and work on Adele, I think that you may be more successful than counting on Adele's vast deep affection for you.

The serial goes on. I'm now in installment seven. The fifth, sixth, and seventh installments are fairly good, but I feel they're not up to the first four, and I've lost the chance I had to write a really major novel. On the other hand, I don't think I could have brought in a really good book in eight installments, and I know I wouldn't have had the strength to go on for twelve. It's been an incredible push because I've had to write figuratively with a locked wrist, since there was no time to explore and follow the kind of incidental bent which two times out of three leads you up a blind alley and then discovers a bigger book within the book. Anyway, I still think it's going to be one of the best books written in a long time.

I saw the Clay-Liston fight, but won't do a piece on it because there hasn't been time. A pity. I think I could have done something good.

I hope Joan's pregnancy is not making her too impatient. I think you're going to love having a kid, and will be much more of a father than you expect. Be prepared, however, for a very bad month or two. I've never known a woman who doesn't go into a deep depression after the birth of her child, particularly the first child. They feel as if the bottom has dropped out of everything, and unless you're prepared for it as something which is as much physiological as psychological, you're going to be miserable.

Norm

P.S. How much do I owe you?

47

TO: FRANCIS IRBY GWALTNEY

*Susie is Susan Mailer Colodro (1949-), the daughter of Mailer and his
first wife Beatrice Silverman (1922-).*

> 142 Columbia Heights
> Brooklyn 1, New York
> May 15, 1964

Dear Fig,

I can't make this as long a letter as I'd like to, because I've just been
working on Installment Eight—I've managed to clear five weeks for it,
and it may turn out to be the longest of them all, because I have to go
on until the book is done. It's not that hard to write a hundred thousand words in eight months—I know you've done it often. But the trick
here is to make them one hundred thousand finished words, and that
makes for strain, because it's hard to relax and get swinging away. So
you don't get many bonuses. It's a little like an actor having to memo-
rize Shakespeare. He can't really relax in the part because of the
demands of the language. So here you can't relax into the serial because of the pressure of time. Anyway, let's see how it all turns out.

Now for some news which may be interesting to you. I've really
missed you and Ecey, Merry Lee and Frank, and I'd like very much to
see you this summer. But why don't you consider this: we're going to
Provincetown for four months, June 1 to September 30, and with any
luck I hope to get a house with four bedrooms. If I do, will you and
Ecey consider coming east for two weeks this summer? Dandy, Betsy,
and Susie are going to be with me for June and part of July, so things
will be a little cramped during that period. But from August 1 I'm sure
we'll have plenty of room, and if you wanted to, you and Ecey can bring
the kids. Provincetown is a fishing village three miles long and two
streets wide, population three thousand in the winter, fifteen thousand
in the summer, but I'd match it in beauty against any European fishing
village I've seen, and it's a marvelous part of the East. Around then it
will be getting pretty hot in Louisiana or Arkansas, and the nights are
cool in Provincetown. So don't argue with me. Find time and find a
way to come up and be our guest for a couple of weeks. You'll have the
best time you've had in years, or I'll consider the trip a failure. And
Frank and Mary Lee will go out of their minds swimming in salt water.
(If my plans work out right, we'll have a house on the beach.)

Mike is now a couple of months old, and his head has slimmed down
from a banana to a lemon. Much to his mother's lack of delight I insist
on calling him Lemon-Head Boiks, since that is indeed his middle name:
Michael Burks Mailer, Bev's father's name being Burks Kendrick Rentz.
Anyway, Mike looks ¾ like Beverly, ¼ like me. He's got my head, my
upper lip, and a nose which gives promise of being just as fat. He looks

48

like a squirrel and he's got a prick on him which makes little girls' eyes open with wonder, carries it in a state of constant erection, as far as I can see. Can you imagine that—a squirrel who's hung?

Give my love to Ecey and let me hear from both of you about this new red-hot idea of mine. A kiss to Mary Lee. You may be the agent who transmits this.

Norm

TO: DON CARPENTER

142 Columbia Heights
Brooklyn 1, New York
June 1, 1964

Dear Don,

A thousand congratulations, and I'm glad that you're now in the same boat with me, one of those high-paid, please-the-public, fink low-brow prostitutes. Wait until you see what awful things happen to your ego when you realize that more people read magazines than novels. Of course, nobody I know reads the *Saturday Evening Post*. Wha'dya do, sell a piece of your cock, schmuck? But down with Lenny Bruce, have a good summer.

I'm just about done with *An American Dream*. There were times when I began to wonder a little, but the seventh installment's pretty good, and the eighth has a bing-bang ending. You didn't think I was going to be squeezing the last drops off my cock at the end, fellow-racketeer—no, I gave them the spatty bit bit spatty be-deet from my old tommy gun. Now we go to Provincetown and I to collapse. The only bad thing about writing a novel in eight months is having to show it once a month. It's like giving a hot fuck to your beloved, and having to pull your cock out eight times for her to inspect it.

If you and your wife are going to work your way through the Kama Sutra backwards, you had better read a few companion volumes: 1) Art is a Schmuck, and 2) Hard as a Hammock. So dot's my koan for today, Clappinger, I mean Don.

Norman

TO: MRS. JOSE CASANOVA

Mrs. Casanova was a Mailer fan. For the length of his career, he has faithfully answered serious letters from admirers. He was late with the long last installment of 19,972 words, which was due at the end of the third week of May for Esquire's *August issue, but turned it in shortly*

49

after this letter. Esquire *had held the presses and saved space for the eighth installment, but it was so long that the second half had to be set in smaller type.*

142 Columbia Heights
Brooklyn 1, New York
June 2, 1964

Dear Mrs. Casanova,

I'm finishing the novel now, so this will excuse, I hope, the briefness of this note, and also will give you in some forty-five or fifty days the opportunity to read the rest of the book, and tell me whether you think it comes together as a novel with overall meaning, or is just an elongated *jeu des mots*. Please give me your reactions to it.

Yours sincerely,
Norman Mailer

TO: MICKEY KNOX

Fred Betah was the first husband of Joan Morales.

142 Columbia Heights
Brooklyn 1, New York
June 2, 1964

Dear Mick,

It's now more than a month after your last letter, and no further news from you, and not a word from Omar Sharif, whom I did see in "Lawrence of Arabia," and did think was marvelous. Incidentally, he's a very handsome but exact version of Fred Betah, so I felt as if I knew him very well. What did Joan think of him?

And when is the baby due? It must be any day now. Send me a telegram when it happens. If it's after June 3, Mickey, send it to me c/o Arlie Sinaiko, 603 Commercial Street, Provincetown, Mass.

Well, I'm finally coming to the end of *An American Dream.* I've finished the last installment rough draft, and I'm giving it the final polish. What a murderous fucking installment this last one has been. I'm in pretty good shape, but of course tense as hell, and all burned out from smoking. I feel just the way a wire must feel after a short circuit. But the book is pretty good, I think, and if it does nothing else, will make me enough money so that I can pay my alimony for a couple of years. I don't think anything changed my life quite so much as losing my loot on the stock market and having to pay Adele that twenty grand a year. It's amazing how I, who was always so impractical, am now making a living.

Incidentally, I'm pretty sure I did receive a letter from you about ten days ago, a typewritten letter, but I've looked all around and can't seem

50

to find it, of all the damn luck. Anyway, in it I seem to remember your asking about the movie of *An American Dream*. It's simple enough. Warner's took an option for twenty grand, against $200,000 if they take it within four months after completion. Some of the newspapers reported it was sold outright at $300,000, but that of course was Hollywood reporting. Anyway, if you get into a situation where you have money to make your movie, run into trouble, and need a few thousand more, I'd probably be able to help you. I'd offer to put up the full twenty-five grand you mentioned in your letter, but I'm likely to clear no more than $100,000 after debts, taxes, what-have-you, and I've got to put most of the money aside so that I can get to work on the big novel.

No news other than work. I've hardly seen a soul in weeks, and spend most of my time pushing a pencil. But this summer we're going to be in Provincetown for four months. Is there any chance you'll be back in the States between June and September? Because if so, I'd sure like you to come up—I think we'd have room to put you up.

Wish Joan a good delivery for me. Bev has been in pretty good shape, and Michael is nothing but a prick. Every time his mother changes his diaper, he gets a hard-on.

Best, and love,
Norm

TO: DIANA ATHILL

Mailer complains here of the way the British edition of his novel is described in the Deutsch catalogue of forthcoming books.

597 Commercial Street
Provincetown, Massachusetts
July 5, 1964

Dear Diana,

On the negative side, I have only a few comments for the catalogue page. I think "evil wife" oversimplifies too much. I think "tragic, tormented, half-evil wife" or something of that ilk might be more satisfactory. Also, "sane love" with Cherry sounds hygienic. "To find some part of his dream of love" might be more what we need. Outside of that, I think it's fine. But I also think we're giving away much too much by saying that An American Dream is so unlike "mannerly British fictions," for it seems to me that the virtuoso aspect of *An American Dream* is that it is so mannered a book. Violent people always are mannerly, or chaos would result if there were not a spectrum of manners in their dealings with each other. Now this has always fascinated the British—[Dashiell] Hammett, [Raymond] Chandler, so forth. But of course the manners they showed there were essentially false ones. The reality is curious and somehow subtler, and I was trying to get toward that reality in *An American Dream*. But I think it would be a serious mistake to abdicate from any claims this novel can make in the dominion of manners, because it is precisely by the play of manners that I've tried to tell the story. One could even go so far perhaps as to argue that the novel is a study of the bizarre, incisive, and very elaborate manners of some of the kinds of people who live in the social worlds and under-worlds of New York. So I think we might emphasize the book is in its way as mannered as a novel by Henry James. What creates the—it is to be hoped—fascinating confusion is that the material is closer to a Mickey Spillane.

By the way, Diana, how do you all feel about the end of the book? There's been not a word about that from Andre [Deutsch] or from you. If you're unhappy, now's the time to talk, because I hope to put in about five to ten thousand words and take out a little of the old, all of this to be accomplished by September 1. Since I'm also going to do the Republican Convention, there'll be only a few weeks for this, probably from August 10 to September 1. But in the month between, there would certainly be time to get your comments. Please believe me, I'm not so delicate as to be afraid of negative comments. And this can go right down to the individual sentences. It's really a good idea to let me know now whatever bothers you and Andre. Of course, if the end is a vast disappointment to you ... But then I hope not. I was so tired by the time I finished I was willing to accept any external verdict that it was very good or very bad. The good remarks I heard were that it was very good, but then it was the agent and publisher who said that, and they're not exactly similar to the critics in their interest. At any rate, give us a reaction.

Best for now,
Norman

TO: PETE HAMILL

Journalist and novelist, Pete Hamill (1935-) has been a friend of Mailer since they met in Chicago in 1962. Eddie Machen, the heavyweight boxer, lost to Floyd Patterson in Stockholm on 5 July 1964. Sammy Taub was a prizefight announcer. Al Aronowitz was a sportswriter. J. F. Powers (1917-1999), the Irish novelist, published Morte D'Urban *in 1962. Gunter Grass (1927-) is a German novelist.*

597 Commercial Street
Provincetown, Massachusetts
July 5, 1964

Dear Pete,

I did something very funny with your suggestion about sending a copy of *The Presidential Papers* to Floyd [Patterson]. Usually, certainly in the old days, I would have moved fast on such a thought. But this time it just didn't feel right. I felt spooked by the whole thing, as if I wouldn't forgive myself if Floyd happened to read the piece and then lost to [Eddie] Machen. Floyd's probably forgotten this, but I sent him some tearsheets of the piece when we were out in Las Vegas, and Sammy Taub said that he delivered them to Floyd personally (which may not be true) but I can tell you that I was glad to hear Floyd had never read it, because I felt spooked by the Las Vegas fight, as if Floyd had read it, and it had gotten him thinking of other things and all of a sudden his mind was somewhere else and he walked in on Sonny at the end of the first minute in that first round. Anyway, Machen is his kind of fighter. If he's going to be able to beat him, I'm sure he'll be able to beat him without any assistance from me, and then maybe would be the time to send it to him.

The gossip about the book and the money it's making is way off. At present there's no movie sale, just an option. And there's a good chance the option won't be picked up because Warner's wants me to change the title and I've told them I don't want to. (It seems audiences will not go to see a movie which has the word American in it. At least, that's what all the money in Hollywood has decided.) No, the book has done well, but the figure is one third as large as you've been reading, and so I'm hardly yet in the ranks of the wealthy. But still, after alimony and taxes, I ought to have at least two years free to myself in which I don't have to sweat the production of each week's bread. I think you're right about the reviews. I think they're going to be murderous, and indeed I'm already half resigned to that. If they're too bad, maybe I'll leave the country in protest, a la Henry James.

Actually, the idea of moving seems tough right now. I've got all my kids with me and we're having a good time up here, we're on the water, which is the place to be in Provincetown. But the thought of moving this menagerie *cum* factory is beyond my ambition. I may get over to England for a couple of weeks during the winter, and if I do and you're still in Dublin, could I fly up to visit for a couple of days, maybe? I've never seen Ireland, and I'd like to very much I think.

Mike is now three and a half months old and a very cute kid, very sweet, and kind of gentle for a boy. And as I said earlier today, wouldn't that just be the ticket if I end up with a son who's a dove. Anyway, the Burks comes from Bev's side, her father's first name was just that. You can tell Ramona that Mike weighs sixteen pounds now, he's about sixteen weeks old.

Finally, give my regards to J.F. Powers if you run into him. I read *Morte D' Urban* a couple of weeks ago, and enjoyed sheer hell out of it. He's not a great writer, and probably never will be, but he sure is good.

Also, say hello to Al when you see him. I ran into Aronowitz at a party for Gunter Grass just about a month ago in New York.

Peter, I haven't seen any of the things you've written, outside of the piece on Spain. If I'd known you were writing for the *Saturday Evening Post,* I'd have kept an eye on the contents week to week.

Best for now,
Norman

TO: EIICHI YAMINISHI

597 Commercial Street
Provincetown, Massachusetts
July 7, 1964

Dear Eiichi,

This is just a quick note. By now, ideally, you've received the last three installments (six, seven, and eight) of *An American Dream,* and so you can think about the book as a whole. Much of the news you have heard about the novel is untrue or inaccurate. For instance, it will not be published in October or November, but in January. Same for England. And it has not been sold to the films. Warner Brothers took an option but of course may decide not to buy it. That of course is all by the bye. The book may make a vast amount of money, it may not—but what it has done is to provide me with sufficient income so that for the next two years I can concentrate on doing the best writing of which I'm capable without fear or wonder how to meet my expenses.

Apart from the fact that this was a commercial book (that is, one of the basic motives for its conception was the desire to make a great deal of money) it is also my attempt to write as good a novel as possible under the circumstances, and as I think you will see, the book, while conventional in many aspects, is also unusual in its "psychic world," and may in this sense go further than any novel I know. Incidentally, I'm going to spend a few weeks this summer making changes in the text. They will be little changes, but numerous ones. For that reason, I would suggest you do not start your translation until the middle of September when I can give you the final copy, unless it should prove necessary to go to work earlier. If that proves the case, we'll have to figure a way to send you the changes. That of course will mean more work for you and more work for me. At any rate, dear Eiichi, my best to you for now, and hope that all is well with your fine family, so many good sons and daughters.

Warmly,
Norman

TO: DIANA ATHILL

Mailer did not revise the serial version of the novel as quickly as he had hoped. He worked on it through the summer and early fall of 1964 in Provincetown, putting it aside for the "long piece" he wrote about the August Republican Convention. Titled "In the Red Light: A History of the Republican Convention in 1964," it appeared in the November issue of Esquire. *Kelly is Barney Oswald Kelly, Deborah's father and Rojack's nemesis in the novel. Mailer had chosen Kelly's name, which eerily echoes that of Lee Harvey Oswald, at least two months before Oswald was killed by Jack Ruby. Mailer continues to believe that the similarity in the names may be more than a coincidence.*

> 597 Commercial Street
> Provincetown, Massachusetts
> August 21, 1964

Dear Diana,

Just the briefest of notes—I'm racing through the mail today, but wanted to tell you that I was delighted you liked the book, and will go through your criticisms along with the ones I received from Dial in the next few weeks, for I plan to have the book in final shape by—at the latest—the middle of September, and hope actually to be ready to go by September 1. In fact the only thing I don't agree with you about is glens and dells. I thought somehow it was right for Kelly—at least I could hear his voice.

I'm working very hard this month on a long piece about the Republican Convention. I was out in San Francisco for the week and since coming back have done just about nothing else. The result is a long piece, 21,000 words, which were very different from the piece on Kennedy and the Democrats, and may have turned out about as well— at least I hope so. My agent wants to try selling it to a British newspaper or magazine as well as *Esquire*. How about *The Observer*? They've approached me in the past.

Incidentally, my folks were delighted with the good care you took of them, and I know appreciated it more than a bit. I don't think the hotel bothered them too much. At a certain point I turned to my mother and said, "Well, after all, you certainly were the youngest girl there," and she gave her full laugh, and her eyes turned very merry for a moment.

All else is well, except for the photograph in *The Observer*. Were you able to obtain prints of it? I really think I'd like to use it for the book, at least for the American edition. If it proves to be one of those little things which are enormously complicated, then I wouldn't want time to be taken on it. After all, one can always get a good photograph if one takes a haircut.

> Excelsior,
> Norman

P.S. Dictating this to Anne, A.B. remarked, "But perhaps the letter was lost in the mail strike." Is that possible?

TO: ROBERT F. LUCID

Longtime professor of English at the University of Pennsylvania, Lucid (1931-) is one of Mailer's closest friends and his authorized biographer. They met at the University of Chicago in 1958 during Mailer's visit there. Lucid edited the first collection of critical essays on Mailer, Norman Mailer: The Man and His Work *(1971). Mailer took Lucid's advice and added a scene between Rojack and the detective, Roberts, in the Dial version of the novel.*

597 Commercial Street
Provincetown, Massachusetts
September 29, 1964

Dear Bob,

We'll be in October 1. Any chance for you, Joanne, and Jackie to visit us shortly after? You know, I ended up following your advice about Roberts. There's a short very odd little scene with him which takes place now after Cherry's death. I believe it's right, but it's a very odd little scene. I'd really like you to see it. I think if you said, "Leave it in," or "Take it out," I would be inclined to obey. At any rate, whether I did it successfully or not—if it's successful while I was writing it, which means it's now impossible for me to judge it, since I'm best on things which are half-successful and so enable me to work them into shape—at any rate, realized or no, your idea was altogether right: it stayed with me all summer. So wouldn't it be fine if I could show it to you now. Listen, what's your phone number? Wouldn't even know how to reach you fast if there were a good party. VaROOM!

Beverly, Annie, Michael all fine.

Best and most,
Norman

TO: DON CARPENTER

597 Commercial Street
Provincetown, Massachusetts
October 5, 1964

Dear Don,

This is just a yeah-man-like-I-liked-your-last-letter letter, because I'm feeling a little written out. I did twenty thousand words on the Republican Convention—did I tell you? And they're going to be in the

November *Esquire*, out toward the end of October. It's pretty good I think and I expect you might enjoy it, what with the local scene and all. Then I spent the rest of the summer getting *An American Dream* into shape. It's a little tighter, stronger, meaner, and it's got a little more gold in it, so I don't know, either I've got a very good novel, like maybe the best book in ten years, or else I've got an incredibly fancy piece of shit. I've worked it too hard to know, but my secretary, Anne Barry, a stuck-up little New Hampshire cunt whom you may have met, is giggling her stuck-up head off as I make this remark. So I have just fired her, and will have to rehire her in the morning—Don, I'm only kidding. Anyhoo, don't bother, as you have suggested you might, to read the installments through, because the book will be out in a couple of months, and it's just sufficiently different in critical little ways so that you'd have to read the book version too.

This is all for now. I'm beat from too much writing, and once again doing all the letters on the same day. But I did want to say one thing, which is for Christ's sake, never to apologize for getting interested or even being an actor on a power scene, no matter how picayune, for that after all is the very protein fat of what we have to write about.

Best for now,
Norman

TO: ANDRE DEUTSCH

The Dial version, delayed several times, appeared on 15 March 1965. Deutsch published the British edition on 26 April. The photograph of Mailer by Anne Barry on the back of the dust jacket of the Dial edition was taken as Mailer shadowboxed with her. Mailer designed the front of the jacket, which superimposes a photograph of Beverly Bentley on the American flag. A different version of the jacket appeared as the cover illustration of the 12 October 1964 Publishers' Weekly. *A double-page advertisement in this number states that the novel would be published in January, but it was delayed while Mailer made additional revisions, including significant changes to the galleys.*

142 Columbia Heights
Brooklyn 1, New York
November 4, 1964

Dear Andre,

I've been meaning to call you each day, but each day I've not remembered until around cocktail time, which of course is bloody midnight for you. Now I've decided to do it with a letter.

Look, quickly, here's the situation. If you're still interested in joint publication—which I think is a good idea, since if the reviews in one country are better than another, the foreign reviews can be used, and if the reception is good in both countries, something can be made of that—at any rate, if you're still interested, Dial has decided not to publish until February 15 (an approximate date). It took me longer on the editing than I expected, their printing schedule took longer than they expected, and suddenly we were rushing to get a book out early for no reason that we could see. So as it stands, final page proofs will be ready in a week to two weeks. I'll get two copies off to you as soon as they exist, I swear. There's no sense in sending you anything any earlier because keeping up with the changes would have made for endless waste for you and for me. I know it's been anything but easy for you to have to wait this way, but I think when you read the book through you'll see that all these changes on which I've been working since June add up to something, the difference I hope between a book which is good and a book which is better than good.

Now for the jacket, I'll send you a copy. I happen to like it quite a bit. It's an odd compelling jacket and quite different from what you saw in *Publishers' Weekly*. That is, the design is essentially the same, but they changed it in certain crucial and disappointing ways for *PW*. In any case, I like the jacket. I hope you'll like it, and I'll also enclose a photograph which I'm going to use for the book jacket.

This is all in a rush, but I know you're waiting for the news, so hasten to dictate this letter.

Best,
Norman

P.S. Three cheers that you're setting the book rather than using offset. I'm really pleased with that.

TO: ESTHER WHITBY

Esther Whitby was a Mailer fan. The Menells were related to the Mailers by marriage.

142 Columbia Heights
Brooklyn 1, New York
December 15, 1964

Dear Mrs. Whitby,

It was agreeable to get your letter, and I rush to answer, because I feel the change you made was not correct. Rojack has been married nine years. It is just that in one place (in the beginning of Chapter 2) he speaks of having spent a year learning something about Deborah, and then in effect having the leisure to consider it for the next eight years. I hope this is the only apparent inconsistency. I have a small uneasy feeling—I'm very bad about these matters—that I may have said in one place or another that they were married "all but nine years," probably for no other reason than that I liked too much the sound of "all but." If that sort of discrepancy does appear here and there, I think that we ought nonetheless to stay with nine, because its sound is sufficiently different from eight so that the cadence of a few sentences might be hurt a bit if we changed. Under the circumstances, we can defend nine as poetic license.

Yes, I guess we are related, by marriage at any rate. But you must be a Menell. I remember meeting Bertha back in 1947, and another Menell, the son or nephew of Slip Menell, about two years ago in New York. Well, when I get to London we'll have to talk about all this.

My best for now,
Norman Mailer

TO: ARNOLD KEMP

Kemp met Mailer in Bellevue Hospital. The existentialism of Jean-Paul Sartre (1905-1980) interested Mailer and he wrote about it in both Advertisements for Myself *and* The Presidential Papers, *although Sartre's existentialism is distinguished from Mailer's by its atheism. Mailer wrote about Barry Goldwater (1909-1998) in his November 1964* Esquire *essay "In the Red Light: A History of the Republican Convention in 1964."*

142 Columbia Heights
Brooklyn 1, New York
December 18, 1964

Dear Arnold,

The last time I wrote to you I thought I was done with the book, but in fact the galleys came back and I saw little sentences here and there that I could improve, so I made some changes. The result: the book will not be out until March. But I've got you on the list, and will send you a copy as soon as they're ready, which ought to be sometime in early February.

You know, when Sartre won the Nobel Prize, it's funny, but we have a different attitude. I think he should have taken it, and the reason I think is that it bugs the bourgeoisie more when people who are against them accept their biggest prizes rather than refuse them. For example, all these years *Life* magazine has been calling Jean-Paul Sartre an "apostle of despair." Now all of a sudden, apostle of despair and Nobel Prize winner. That makes it harder for them to bullshit people. I believe in taking honors because if you use them properly they arm you. Some day if there were something really big going on and one wanted to write a letter to the *New York Times*, a mean stinging letter, and get it printed, there'd be just that much more leverage.

You know, another thing I disagree with you on is [Barry] Goldwater's rights stand. I do think, believe it or not, that that was the main reason people voted against him. It's not that white America loves black America, but what you've got to understand is that even without love there can still be guilt. There is a kind of gnawing guilt that pervades practically every white man's attitude by now, a guilt they want to get rid of even though they fear the Negro, and I think they've come to the point now where they recognize that the only way to get rid of this guilt or at least begin to get rid of this guilt is to begin to give the Negro some of his basic minimal legal rights, and I think they did react against Goldwater for that reason. At any rate, this election cheered me up. For the first time I began to feel there might be something to this country, that maybe we're a little more on the ball than not. Because secretly I felt that the first time some real slick bigot like Goldwater came along, he was going to stampede everybody. So for once it wasn't so bad to know that I was wrong.

I know I can't get to see your plays, because as I understand you're not allowed to send them out, but I wish there was a way. I'd like to see the work you're doing. Merry Christmas for now, ha ha, and happy New Year, yea, yea, yea.

Best,
Norman

TO: MICKEY KNOX

Mailer continues to be interested in the existentialism of the German philosopher Martin Heidegger (1889-1976). Robert Frank (1924-) is a well-known photographer, filmmaker and member of the 1960s counterculture. Charles Frances Eitel is the movie producer in Mailer's third novel, The Deer Park. *Irving Shulman was a novelist whose agent was also Scott Meredith. Maria Consuelo Morales was the mother of Adele and Joan Morales.*

142 Columbia Heights
Brooklyn 1, New York
December 18, 1964

Dear Mickey,

Once again I'm banging my way through seventy or eighty letters, so there's no pleasure in writing to anybody. I think [Martin] Heidegger, in speaking of matters like being and authenticity, also discusses the nothingness of a great many daily events—the matter of pursuing activities which are tasteless, joyless, probably not even necessary, and pervasive. And letter-writing, of course, [is] all a large part of that nothingness for me. This is by way of apology for the flatness of my letters. By the time I finish a letter to you, I always feel as if I'd let you down in some indefinable way.

Now as for the famous Robert Frank letter, the one you may or may not have received, I'm so confused by now that I'm going to send you my carbon of it, and you'll then be able to decide for yourself whether or not the original ever caught up with you.

I'm glad you liked the Republican Convention piece. It's amusing, but reactions to it here have been more positive than anything I've done since *The Naked and the Dead.* I think the piece is good, but I wonder if it's really so good as everyone says, or is buoyed up somewhat by the intense hatred most people feel for Goldwater. This is all very fine, the approval, I mean, because it puts me a tiny bit back in fashion, which I can use for *An American Dream.* The advance word out on the novel, you see, is that I've written a stinker. Which of course burns my ass. If it's a stinker, I'm off my moorings. I don't want to say too much now, but I've reworked that book as carefully as if I were giving a lovely lady my loveliest, and I think ... well, read it for yourself. I'll get a copy to you as soon as I can. In fact I think I'll send you two copies so you can hand one around.

Give my regards to [Orson] Welles, and tell him I said it's a great pity he's not in the theater any more, because I always wanted him to do Charles Francis Eitel. Also, if you've got a copy of *The Presidential Papers*, and it's feasible, tell Welles that I'd like him to read "The Metaphysics of the Belly," where he will doubtless agree with me that he is no longer alone—there are now two great minds in the world. I'm kidding, Mickey, don't put yourself out on this last one.

Listen, I don't get it. Why don't you get a babysitter? As I remember, labor in Spain, housemaids, babysitters, etc., is unbelievably inexpensive. Certainly it will cost you a lot less than taking care of Maria Morales' passage and incidental expenses. Besides, I don't think you know what you're getting in for. It's one thing to dominate her when you're around, and it's another thing to dominate her when you're on the set and she's sitting around chatting at home with Joanie. So think twice, amigo.

Listen, these are my plans. I'm going over to England for the publication of *An American Dream,* and will be there a week or two. Maybe I'll take on a trip to Italy or Spain for another week or two. That depends on a hundred different things—whether I go alone, with Beverly, with Beverly and Michael, all sorts of things that are too hard to answer at the moment. But anyway, I'm just about positive I won't be over before that. So probably I'll be seeing you in Rome rather than in Spain. Or maybe we can meet at a ski resort. There are enough possibilities, aren't there.

Hey, one bit of news. Irving Shulman has the same agent I do, and wanted to meet me. We couldn't get together, but did talk on the phone, and of course he asked all about you, and listened with interest, and I get the impression he'd like to hear from you. So if you're in the mood, drop him a letter in care of Scott Meredith, 580 Fifth Avenue, New York.

Give Valentina a kiss for me, and tell her to watch out for Michael, because he's a real prick—every time I throw a punch at him, he just busts out laughing.

Love,
Norm

TO: BILL MCLAUGHLIN

McLaughlin was a Mailer fan.

142 Columbia Heights
Brooklyn 1, New York
December 18, 1964

Dear Bill McLaughlin,

Going through old mail, I came across your nice long letter of August 19. Well, sir, you are the fortunate recipient of prompt response.

Actually, it's so late in the day that I think I'd better use this occasion to wish you Merry Christmas, and let it go at that. I did enjoy your letter, though; particularly the criticisms of the last installment of *An American Dream*. I worked the book up some since then, you know, and while it's superficially the same book, I think it's a different book. Tightening prose is like tightening a drum: you get better sound. If you happen to read the book when it comes out, let me know your reaction. I'd be interested.

Yours,
Norman Mailer

TO: VIRGINIA D. MANGRUM

Mrs. Mangrum was still another Mailer fan.

142 Columbia Heights
Brooklyn 1, New York
December 21, 1964

Dear Mrs. Mangrum,

As I wrote to a Negro friend of mine just yesterday, I decided this year to lay down the White Man's Burden and send out no Christmas cards. But of course it's still agreeable to receive them. I'd held off from answering your last long letter because there was so much in it which was interesting and generous and large that I didn't want to reply too stingily. At the same time I kept working on *An American*

Dream, I really finished it off just yesterday. It's a curious book. I worked the hell out of the last chapter and gave a lot to the others. Yet when you read the book you may not be able to detect the difference, for the structure is exactly the same. But nearly every sentence was worked on nearly every which way, sometimes leaving it alone, or going back to leaving them alone, sometimes changing a preposition, sometimes cutting a phrase or adding one, but I felt more like a musician than a writer, as if I had a very good kettle drum which was devilish to tune. I think I'm guilty of having used this image in several letters before, and if I were a Catholic I would now cross myself against the possibility that I used exactly the same image in my last letter to you. But my memory tells me that I did not, and so it might have been wiser to have presented the metaphor as an original rather than a copy. However, caution comes upon me as I get older. I'd make a good general now, quartermaster, I fear, and not the Marines.

Listen, Mrs. M., I'm glad you mention your husband, because I'm certain he must be a marvelous man if he is both a Marine Corps General and husband to a wife as rich and varied in her parts as yourself, and still so very much in love with her husband. I must say, madam, they did not make generals like that in the Army. But in fact the name Mangrum means something to me, and I have such a pulverized memory, I am not quite sure what. Probably he's one of the famous Marine Corps generals and I'm just an ass not to know the campaign and the battle. At any rate, famous, marvelous, or more modest than that. He must be okay to meet, and I look forward to meeting him at any time when I could meet you. Do you ever come up to New York? If so, perhaps you would come over to Brooklyn for a drink. I've got the best view of New York of anyone who lives in the city, and I know my wife would enjoy meeting you. But listen, this is all in the future, I fear. At the present I'm looking forward to sending you a copy of *An American Dream* in about a month. Between us, I'm just a little tickled with the book, because no matter it's larger merits or lack of them, I worked the surface of this book harder than anything I've ever written and so feel at last there's a certain craftsmanship to something I've done. To me it purrs a little now. It's a bitch of a book, at least I think so. If you don't like it, or are a good bit disappointed, my god, I'll respect you for saying so after reading all these fine words about me by me.

Since you were so nice as to send me a picture, let me send one back. The gentleman in the front is my son, Michael. Six months old at the time, now nine months, born on St. Patrick's Day, Michael Burks Mailer.

Let me wish a Merry Christmas to your family,
Norman Mailer

TO: EIICHI YAMINISHI

Mailer's comment about adding "a piece" to the novel is in reference to the Japanese edition. As he indicates, he is satisfied with the length of the novel, which he had just finished cutting by almost 2,000 words. The Dial edition contains 96,910 words; the Esquire version has 98,796. Warner Brothers paid Mailer $200,000 for the screen rights to the novel.

142 Columbia Heights
Brooklyn 1, New York
January 27, 1965

Dear Eiichi,

I thought in answer to your letter of January 18, I would send you a note about the literary style of *An American Dream*. It's a complex style with very many difficulties in it but I thought a key might be of use to you in the translation. So now to begin with—and this is not important—the book is written not so much in my style as in Rojack's and he has an elegant view. He tells the story somewhat elegantly, but there is a subtle tone to this because the elegance is not his naturally by birth or by early family training but is rather an elegance he has acquired in his life and more particularly by being married to Deborah for nine years, and so for that reason there are flaws in the manner, subtle flaws, subtle roughnesses, departures in tone so to speak, which is to say that Rojack tends to talk like the person he is talking to. If you notice carefully he is one way with Deborah, another with the police, still another with Cherry. Oddly enough he is probably most himself when he is with Ruta because while the style of speech then becomes grand and somewhat metaphorical, there is a vast irony in its mood. She after all is a bit of an upstart; Rojack is a complete upstart and so he enjoys himself enormously when he is with her. Now of course I don't want these notes to bother you too much. I'm all too aware that it is never easy to transpose a subtlety from one language to another, but I thought these few comments might serve as a guide to some of the almost invisible shifts in style in the book.

I'm a little concerned that *An American Dream* is going to have a piece added to it to make up a suitable length for the book. I think this tends to diminish the respect people might feel for a novel as a complete novel. It is after all a longer book than half the novels which appear here in a year. Is there no possibility that they could use larger type? See if it is possible to discuss this matter with the editors of *World Literature*.

Yes, the news about the movie is true. Warner Brothers has bought it and we are making a movie of it sometime in the future. At first they almost didn't buy it because they were unhappy with the title. They wanted me to change the title to "Strong Are the Lonely." Do you know, Eiichi, they are even more fantastic than what one has written about them. I, of course, refused and subsequently they bought the book. Don't you know that if I had accepted their title, they would doubtless have decided finally not to buy the book. The secret reason for the dislike of *An American Dream* turns out to be that the films with the word "American" in them do poorly at the box office, not in Asia, not in Europe, but here, right here. It seems America is tired of hearing about America. What a curious nation we are. Sometimes I think we are coming out of a long illness.

All best to you and to your family,

Warmly,
Norman

TO: DIANA ATHILL

Mailer's extreme dissatisfaction with the dust jacket of the Deutsch edition may have led to the elimination of "the gentlemen in the car wreck" (one half of the painting) from the back of the dust jacket of the British book club edition that followed the Deutsch edition.

142 Columbia Heights
Brooklyn 1, New York
February 25, 1965

Dear Diana,

The jacket aroused my fury on two counts. 1) The girl on the cover doesn't bear the remotest resemblance to Deborah, Cherry, or even Ruta. The result, so far as I am concerned, is that people will be imagining a woman who does not correspond to any of the women in the book. You know, when you spend a lot of time working on a character, trying to etch their outlines clearly, it's not agreeable to see the work overturned by a gimmick. I really wish I'd been consulted on the jacket.

Which brings me to the second point. 2) I don't mind not having a photograph of myself on the book, but the gentleman in the car wreck on the back of the jacket is unmistakably a dog-faced version of this particular pen. Now Diana, I need that about as much as you do. 3) (I find there's a third objection after all) That is the value of the jacket altogether. It's a most interesting painting, not terribly good, not altogether good, not altogether bad, but it manages to indicate symbolically just about every element of the book, which means that people are going to be picturing the book through the artist's eyes as much as through mine, and that's going to result in a doubling of the effect which may prove fatal. It's one thing for me to create an atmosphere of horror, it's another to drench the reader in a state of horror before he begins to read the book. If you're going to dare playing an entire

65

composition in the key of C, it's not necessarily wise to strike thirty chords in the key of C before you begin. Now I grant you the jacket is the first of it's kind, etc., etc., and I'm sure that everyone in the book industry will notice it, and people in the book stores will notice it (of course if they do not look closely they will think it is the jacket of a paperback book) but what the jacket will not accomplish is a deepening of respect for the qualities of the book and that I insist is the single factor which will prove fatal. To push a novel by Norman Mailer as a best seller can only draw the wrath of the critics. Get a string of bad reviews, and you're dead. This has been my argument from the beginning. It has not been listened to and I just [think] you're all not dead wrong, though certainly I think you are.

Now one thing I must insist on. I want the photograph which Anne Barry took of me to be the sole photograph released for publicity. It's a picture which in my opinion fits the book more closely than any other photograph I've ever had taken, and for that reason I want no other.

Best for now, Diana, and we'll talk about my visit after we've cleared the air a little on these matters.

Norman

TO: RICHARD KLUGER

Kluger was an editor at the literary supplement, Book Week. *Mailer was responding, in part, to his request for a list of the books that most influenced him. Tom Wolfe (1931-), novelist and New Journalist, wrote a negative review of* An American Dream *that appeared in* Book Week *on 14 March 1965. Philip Rahv (1908-1973), the literary critic, wrote his negative review for the 25 March 1965 number of the* New York Review of Books, *then and now edited by Robert B. Silvers (1929-). Granville Hicks (1901-1982) was the literary editor of The* Saturday Review, *where on 20 March 1965 he gave the novel a negative review, suggesting that it was a literary hoax. Mailer called him "predictable Hicks" in a review of Norman Podhoretz's memoir,* Making It, *in* Partisan Review, *spring 1968.*

142 Columbia Heights
Brooklyn 1, New York
March 22, 1965

Dear Dick,

Thank you for your letter, which was a good one. There are no hard feelings. All you can ever ask of a book review editor is that he offers you a fair to good draw on the reviewer. And in advance I would have said Tom Wolfe was a fair choice. The *New York Review [of Books]* is the one I'm irritated at. Because [Robert B.] Silvers must have known

(everyone else in New York did) that my work has been anathema to
Philip Rahv for years.

Here's the list. I'm not very happy with it, and I'm not sure you're
doing the right thing. It's the sort of poll that tends to reinforce a
literary establishment. My opinions go into the hopper with Granville
Hicks'—what does that accomplish? Since there are more Hicks, he
thrives on this sort of poll and ultimately I perish. Perhaps not personally, i.e., my "stock" can remain high, but my power to influence opinion
has to be diminished by setting up a College of Electors of this sort.

Sincerely,
Norman

TO: DIANA ATHILL

*Alexander King was a humor writer and raconteur who appeared regu-
larly on television talk shows. George Weidenfeld was a British publisher. Weidenfeld and Nicolson succeeded Andre Deutsch as Mailer's
British publisher in 1967 and published five of his books through 1971.*

142 Columbia Heights
Brooklyn 1, New York
March 23, 1965

Dear Diana,

Just a quick note. Our letters keep seeming to cross in the mail, and
doubtless will again. What I'm curious about and what I'd like to know
more of is what ideas you and Andre have about my showing up in
London. I think it would be a mistake to repeat the thing we did last
time with Advertisements. We had something like four or five television or radio shows packed into a few days, a mass press conference
which produced no news whatsoever, and in general I ran around like a
whore after a hot buck and probably sold fifty copies. In this country
I've noticed that the same thing results, with the exception of anoma-
lies like Alexander King. Going on television does not sell books—in
fact I have a feeling it tends to hinder the sale of books. So long as an
author remains a bit of a mystery and a touch inaccessible the reader
must enter the pages of his work in order to satisfy his curiosity.
Seeing a man on television is all too likely to produce the thought, "Oh
well, he's not so different from you or me."

On this novel I've done no television here at all, no radio, just a few
interviews and one press conference, yet the literary publicity has been
intense, front page reviews, etc., and the book looks off to a good start.
So this is what I would propose: if my presence in London is going to do
any good I think we must try to disarm the literary establishment.
Perhaps we can have a few slick interviews with first-rank intellectuals

who are very hostile to my work but who would on general reputation give me a fair show. Or perhaps an open debate in Festival Hall or some place much smaller and much more suitable with some bright blade from *The New Statesman* or wherever, who detests *An American Dream* and would like the chance to cut me up in public. I think a packed house of that sort, even if it were five hundred people would give the novel its real and best kind of publicity, which is intensive talk in the parlors and the salons. (Incidentally, in an open public debate I don't give bloody bugs if the debater is a dirty fellow—it's just that he's got to be formidable or there's no real action.) That, and if it's possible, a smasher of a party where we try to out-Weidenfeld George—admittedly an impossible task—is my idea of what to do. I don't want under any circumstances, I repeat, to go in for a killing round of stupid empty television appearances in which I'm supposed to come in like a prize bull and stamp my foot. Now, Diana, most simply, if that isn't agreeable to you and to Andre, then I'd really rather not come this trip, for there are many things to do here, including a new book to get started, and these excursions, while they could not be more enjoyable, nevertheless eat up the weeks. So let me know. But please let me know quickly.

Incidentally I have a man who could set up a debate of the sort I propose so if the promotional aspects are bothersome, let me know about that too.

As for the jacket, I'll fulminate no more until I see you, except to say that your letter is a touch ingenuous Diana. The artist says that he was trying to draw Rojack, and who, my pet, do you think most people think Rojack is supposed to be—Albert Einstein?

Yours ever and forever,
Norman

TO: ALAN EARNEY

The New York Times *review Mailer refers to was that of Conrad Knickerbocker, appearing on 14 March 1965. Three of the most positive reviews were by Joan Didion (1934-) in* National Review *on 20 April 1965, by John W. Aldridge in* Life *on 19 March 1965, and by Leo Bersani in the* Partisan Review, *fall 1965. The reviews of the novel did split fairly evenly in the major periodicals, but those in smaller publications across the country were three or four to one, negative to positive.*

142 Columbia Heights
Brooklyn 1, New York
March 23, 1965

Dear Alan,

Let me just send you a copy directly of *An American Dream,* you're certainly welcome to it, and I'll call Grace Bechtold and ask her to hold off on buying one for you.

As for the rest, the reviews have gone oddly on the book. About half have been poor, the other half quite good, but the poles are extreme, everything from "the most important novel written since the war" to "the worst literary hoax of the century." But indeed, as you can guess, I did like the *Times* review.

Best for now,
Norman

TO: JASON EPSTEIN

Epstein (1928-) was the longtime editorial director at Random House, where he was Mailer's editor after Mailer left Little, Brown for Random House in 1984. He is also a founder of the New York Review of Books *and the Library of America. Stanley Edgar Hyman wrote a negative review of* An American Dream *for* The New Leader, *appearing on 15 March 1965.*

142 Columbia Heights
Brooklyn 1, New York
March 25, 1965

Dear Jason,

Your letter was fine, and I'm glad you wrote it to me, for it was clear as well, and so helps to explain why many people don't like the book. I'll not try to answer it here except to say that Rojack is neither mad nor sane, but in that extreme state of fatigue and emotional exhaustion where the senses are crystal clear and paranoia substitutes its vertical salience for the horizontal measure of daily reason, and everything takes place somewhere between a fever and a dream. If the action is big enough, one could even feel clear-headed and purposeful in the midst of all this. I think I may have made the error of not emphasizing this condition, of even not writing a small essay about what it was like. It is, after all, not insanity but an existential state, but I may have been wrong in assuming that people would recognize it as equivalent to some kind of a crisis in their own lives. Philip [Rahv], after all, and Stanley [Edgar] Hyman, seem to give no sense at all of knowing what it is like to be on a three-day bat with something awful behind you and something fearful coming up. One thing is certain so far. This novel has not two bits worth of attraction for intellectuals, our kind of intellectuals, which leads me to suspect that it is either considerably better or considerably less good than I think it is.

Sincerely,
Norman

TO: DON CARPENTER

Carpenter's positive review has not been located.

142 Columbia Heights
Brooklyn 1, New York
March 25, 1965

Dear Don,

I read your review with interest. First of all because it was agreeable to read, second because you said a few things I found fascinating, and third because it was interesting to see how they rearranged it and fucked it up in the newspaper. That opened a door into the world of book review editors and gave a hint of why all book reviews end up reading the same. The reviews in general have been not too bad on *An American Dream,* which is to say they broke about two good, three bad in the important places, and about one good, three bad in the out of town reviews. But the bad reviews were lively and the book seems to be off to a start. I find I hardly care. I've been in a post partum for months, not a deep one, no gloom in this, just a sense of personal flatness. For the first time in years I feel no desire to write the great American novel. It doesn't seem important. I don't seem important. And I'm bored with myself—that's an emotion I haven't felt in years. But it seems to me I spent my last letter complaining in just this fashion, and twice is enough for the best of pen pals. So let me hasten to add that I'll have my secretary call Bob Mills so that he can send the novel on to me and you can be certain I'll be looking forward to this. I'll let you know as soon as I read it, but of course that may not be for several weeks, since I'm off to Alaska April 1 for a few days of action back and forth in the sparkling halls of Greater Northern America.

Best for now,
Norman

TO: DIANA TRILLING

Trilling (1905-1996) was a literary critic and wife of the Columbia professor and man of letters, Lionel Trilling (1905-1975). Her 1962 essay, "The Radical Moralism of Norman Mailer," which appeared in Encounter *in November 1962, is perhaps the most intelligent examination of Mailer's work through* Advertisements for Myself. *Mailer did meet Iris Murdoch (1919-1999) during his visit to England. William Faulkner (1897-1962) was then and now considered to be one of the greatest novelists of the century. Gilles de Rais (1404-1440) was a Marshall of France during the Hundred Years War. Accused of satanic beliefs, he confessed to torturing and killing over 100 children and was*

70

executed. E.M. Forster (1879-1970) wrote a series of novels of English social life in a crisp, ironic style.

142 Columbia Heights
Brooklyn 1, New York
March 25, 1965

Dear Diana,

It's perfect, but after all our talk about how reliable I am, I now pick up the pen (what a metaphor this has become) to tell you that we must go ahead and make plans for my appearance at Oxford even though I may never get to England at all. (That will touch you, darling, to be so genteel and fucking liberal) but you see, I'm having a disagreement at the moment with my British publisher. I don't like the jacket, I don't like the blurb, both of which of course they had to do themselves, and I told them I won't come to England unless we can agree on the kind of publicity. Knowing Andre Deutsch, he will probably want me to go on a round of television and radio appearances, and since I don't do that in New York for a book, I don't see any reason to do it in London. So I have posed other possibilities to him, and now must wait to see if he will agree. Odds are much better than even, however, that I'll be in England, the main reason being that I want to go. So look, let's set a date, I leave it to you, any time after the 23rd, except perhaps publication day, which is something like the 26th or 27th —a phone call to Andre Deutsch in London (Langham 2746-9) will establish the day, and then let me know which day you've chosen. It will be yours.

Now what I'd like ideally is a dinner for eight at your house and then perhaps a few more people in afterward. One can't possibly get to talk to sixteen or twenty people at dinner by any method known to man, and the Senior Common Room, while appealing to the novelist in me, and very suitable and exciting if it should come to pass, promises still less in the way of a delight than dinner for eight in the charming small house you seem to possess. Surely even at Oxford people have been known to drop in after dinner. Isn't that remotely possible? I have only one firm request: you must get Iris Murdoch for dinner. I loved her novel, The Severed Head, and have always wanted to meet her since.

The reception of *An American Dream* has been—believe it if you can—more schizophrenic than anything of mine which preceded it. I've gotten the very best and the very worst reviews I've ever received. John Aldridge of all people, writing in Life, of all the places, said in effect that I was doing the most important writing in the country since [William] Faulkner. Stanley Edgar Hyman in *The New Leader* said it was a dreadful novel. Philip Rahv detested it, so and so loved it. As you can guess, I've enjoyed all this secretly very much, because no vice of mine could be greater than my desire to create a sensation and be forever talked about. Sometimes I wonder, beloved, if I am the ghost of some long-dead London beauty. Well, well, I expect the British will give

71

me good whipping with the thinnest strings of leather for the outrages I've committed in the name of literature. But when you feel in the mood, you must write me what you think of the book, even if you don't like it at all, although I suspect you might just like it, it's an extraordinary novel in its funny fashion, extraordinary, that is, in what it does with the art of the novel, whether for good or ill. It's as if Gilles de Rais had captured the style of E.M. Forster and was running amok with it. So far of course none of the critics have had even the remotest notion that the real debating ground of *An American Dream* is precisely on how it does and does not contribute to the grand art of the novel but I get them so poisonous and upset they can't think straight, and that always tickles my devil, for there is no sight in all the world quite so funny as an intellectual who is too agitated to think. They are then like elephants without a trunk, nothing but hippopotami.

Love,
Norman

TO: DIANA TRILLING

142 Columbia Heights
Brooklyn 1, New York
April 6, 1965

Dear Diana,

Just a racing note. I'm arriving in England the morning of the twentieth, and my business, much as it is, will probably be done by the 27th. So the 28th would probably be better for me than the 30th for the simple reason that I may have just two weeks in Europe and so would like to visit other places. If it's generally the same to you, I'd appreciate it then if you'd make it the 28th or the 29th, but if there's a particular reason for the 30th, then by all means, that's when we'll have it. And I'll plan to spend the night. Incidentally, I still don't know if Beverly will be with me then. She's going to be in Europe for a week of the two and a half weeks I'll be there, but just which part isn't too certain yet. If you're thinking about seating arrangements, I suggest that you assume she'll be with me. If she's not, it would perhaps be possible to get some fine lady on short notice. And if not, we'll all weather the damage.

Forgive the mechanical concentration of this, and the lack of newer news, but I wanted to get it off to you in a hurry.

Norman

P.S. If you haven't answered Jerry Agel's letter yet, then don't. He puts out a monthly publisher's newsletter which is filled with gossip, very little of it nasty or vicious, but I know for certain you would not want any answer you might give to Granville Hicks to appear there. And if you have written to him already, then drop him a line that you would not wish your letter used for publication. One thing more. Please don't bring my name into this. Agel did a long piece on me and treated me reasonably well, and he would be hurt and probably vindictive if he knew I had warned you. But I know how much pain any remarks of yours printed in a newsletter sort of literary magazine would cause you, so I take the unnatural step of working just this much behind the man's back.

All for now. I can't tell you how much I look forward to seeing you and Lionel again.

P.P.S. Tell Lionel that whether he ends up liking or not liking *An American Dream*, I respect him for not deciding immediately. Finally one critic has recognized that the book is not to be taken by storm and hung high or garlanded on the instant.

TO: DONALD KAUFMANN

Kaufmann (1927-) was a professor at the University of Alaska, Fairbanks, who became friendly with Mailer when he spoke at the University in April 1965. In 1969 he published one of the first major critical studies of Mailer, Norman Mailer: The Countdown (The First Twenty Years). *The Christopher Lasch (1939-1994) book Mailer refers to is* The New Radicalism in America, 1889-1963: The Intellectual as a Social Type *(1965).*

> 142 Columbia Heights
> Brooklyn 1, New York
> April 20, 1965

Dear Don,

Just a line to tell you that I love you, and what a fine time we had. So good that it sets up looking forward to the next one. Incidentally, I found when I came home a book written by a man named Christopher Lasch which will be coming out in a couple of weeks, published by Knopf. I can't remember the title, but the subject is a history of intellectual radicalism in America over the last hundred years, and a portion of the last chapter is devoted to your favorite subject for thesis. Lasch didn't have anything to say which rang any big bells for me, and like many before him, he does his best to flatten nuances and make me sound twice as assertive as ever. But the chapter is finally harmless enough. I mention it only because you may wish to include it in your bibliography. Also keep an eye out for the April 20 issue of *The National Review*. To my absolute amazement, there's a rave by Joan Didion on *An American Dream*. And nicely written too, by God.

Give my best to Cheryl, tell her I'm sorry I didn't get a chance to talk to her anymore than I did, and keep slugging, you old fuck of a rabbi.

> Your fellow-alumnus from Heidelberg,
> Old Walk-on-Eggs Norm

TO: JOHN W. ALDRIDGE

John W. Aldridge (1922-) became friends with Mailer in 1951 shortly after Aldridge's After the Lost Generation: A Study of Writers of Two Wars *appeared earlier that year. It contains the first major appreciation of Mailer's work; Mailer wrote an introduction to the 1985 reprint. Aldridge went on to write extensively about Mailer, including reviews of most of his books. Elizabeth Hardwick (1916-) wrote a scolding review that appeared in* Partisan Review *in the spring 1965 number. Richard Poirier (1925-) wrote a very warm review of the novel in* Commentary, *June 1965. In 1972 he published* Norman Mailer, *generally considered to be the most perceptive study of the first half of Mailer's career. William Phillips (1907-2002) was the longtime editor of* Partisan Review.

142 Columbia Heights
Brooklyn 1, New York
April 23, 1965

Dear Jack,

I've held off sending you a batch of reviews, because there seemed no order to most of it. Just New York, dependably, whenever a review was done by someone who lived in New York, the review was bad. There is of course no vast mystery to this. The book was around in serial form for eight months and every literary mind in New York had an opportunity to test his message on every other literary mind, so the intellectual establishment was all bad. Philip Rahv bad, Elizabeth Hardwick in *Partisan Review*, Stanley Edgar Hyman in *The New Leader*, so it will go. Only Richard Poirier in *Commentary* will be good, and that's not out until June. Also, grand surprise, *National Review* had a rave done by Joan Didion, who writes very nicely. At any rate, I'm getting together a batch of duplicates, and I'll send them off with this letter to you. But could you send them back after you've glanced through them, for I think then I'll be mailing the same set on to my daughter in Mexico. Finally, I decided to take out an ad in *Partisan Review*. Elizabeth Hardwick's review was so bad that I decided to oppose it with yours. Originally I planned to use your entire review on two pages, but William Phillips decided that was impossible because of the smallness of the print. And so he cut a couple of hundred words out. I just hope he did the job well. I wasn't here at the time, I was in Alaska, giving— what else—a lecture. And so was unable to see the copy before the deadline. He's conscientious, however, and so it should be all right. Although I must say cutting that piece of yours is not so easy.

The book received such violently opposed reviews that—forgive this weighted metaphor—it was as if the intellectual crust of the nation were suffering a seismographic fault. It was not just the virulence of the bad reviews, except they weren't good on their own terms, and usually they are. The put-down was declarative rather than analytical;

the weight of the indictment seemed to be placed by most New York intellectuals on the improbability of the plot, which is of course the given. That the narrative clichés were chosen precisely because I felt they had been despised so long that a novelistic magic had returned to them seems not to have occurred to Rahv and Co. And so the tone of their reviews is puzzled, irritable, full of loud statement and bad faith. Like an uncle displeased with a nephew and profoundly worried. But I go on too long. You've probably seen most of these reviews yourself, and the ones I send from the smaller papers will prove amusing I hope.

Beverly and I went off this week to Provincetown to pick a house. We'll be there four months I think, and if you're in Nantucket we'll get a chance to visit, for we know a man in Harwichport with a power boat. And so could reach you in two and a half hours door to door. Or if you have a boat, come visit us. We could pick you up in Harwichport. Nantucket after all is a place where people go to work. Provincetown is for sport. Naturally I choose Provincetown for work. At any rate, say hello to Leslie and my regards to your four-year-old. The one-year-old is now somewhat less of a prick. I attribute this to the civilizing influence of his father.

Best and all, Jack,
Norman

P.S. I don't think we have a chance of a snowball in hell, but I'm asking my agent to talk to Jack Warner about having you on for a technical advisor.

TO: MOOS MAILER

Paddy was an English friend of Moos.

142 Columbia Heights
Brooklyn 1, New York
April 23, 1965

Dear Moos,

Well, the news about Paddy was awful, but not altogether a surprise, not even on the first time, some months ago, when you wrote about how bad his condition was, because on the night we met him, in the middle of all the gaiety and great fun of the evening, that cough of his would go off like a string of bombs, and there was this grave-diggers sense in the air of all the deep flesh being torn from its circuits. He was a little haunted that night, as if he knew he had forty more good evenings, or just about, and perhaps that added to the intensity of the occasion. I remember about two in the morning we were drinking in a little bar in Brooklyn, and Paddy decided he wanted to order caviar and champagne for Beverly. But the bar, which was a pretentious little affair run by an Italian who's bartender, head waiter, cook, dishwasher, and lawyer in his spare time, didn't have any caviar, just little Italian hors d'oeuvres, some little pieces of dough and anchovy and tomato paste. So just to josh him, for we'd been teasing each other a little to keep the salt in our good mood, I leaned over to Paddy and said, "You promised me caviar, and all I got was a pizza pie." Well, his eyes flashed. You would have thought I stuck a harpoon in him. For a moment I thought I'd blown the evening. And in fact I shook it, he was so hurt. So then I realized almost too late what a perfectionist he was.

Anyway, my dear, I've written a letter to his wife, as you can see by the enclosure. And if she's agreeable to showing it to you, which I'm certain she will be, I think you'd be interested to read it. It's one of the very few times that I've written a letter of condolence without feeling as if I'd given away a piece of the immortal substance.

Well, *An American Dream* has been out about a month, and has received the very best and the very worst reviews of anything I've ever written. Some of the critics screamed and gnashed their teeth. Some could hardly contain themselves at the over-developments apparently secreted in my nose, some wrote as if they would not get a good night's sleep until they caught me in an alley, and some were generous beyond belief. John Aldridge in *Life* magazine said the writing was better than anything since the best of [William] Faulkner. That was how it went. At present the book is selling fairly well, though not extraordinarily. It's very hard to tell because something like 30 thousand copies are out in the bookstores, and a book that is #1 on the best seller list sometimes sells no more than two or three thousand a week. At any rate the book is #8 on the *Times* list and was reported first at Brentano's, the largest bookstore here, so it's much too early to know just how well it will do. In about two months the answer may be in.

Love,
Norman

TO: JOHN W. ALDRIDGE

142 Columbia Heights
Brooklyn 1, New York
June 8, 1965

Dear Jack,

This is just a line, not a proper letter, to tell you that we'll be up in Provincetown by the time you get this letter. The phone number will be 1424, and our address is 607 Commercial Street. My plans are simple. I'm going to work Monday to Friday and have fun on weekends. So feel ready to come any weekend at all. With a little warning we're bound to have an extra room.

Best and best,
Norman

P.S.   I was not happy with the cuts William Phillips made, they broke the cadence of your style. So I called him up in a huff and he's going to reprint your piece in toto in the next issue.

TO: JOHN WILLIAM CORRINGTON

Corrington wrote a favorable review of the novel in the Chicago Review *(No. 18) 1965. It is unclear what novel Mailer is referring to in the fourth sentence.*

142 Columbia Heights
Brooklyn 1, New York
June 8, 1965

Dear Mr. Corrington,

   I mislaid your letter and didn't come across it again until today, and that was annoying. I didn't want you to think you'd get no answer from me. Now the best time for answering is gone. I'm starting work on a novel soon so starting this week I'm going to be acknowledging mail rather than replying. But look, in any case I can hardly tell you that I thought you were or were not on the right track. That would break the game of criticism, for criticism consists of the critic assuming an authority which he knows in his own heart cannot be authoritative, and that's the fun of it. So I try never to go over a piece of criticism with the critic. I limit myself to saying I enjoyed reading it or didn't enjoy reading it, and obviously I enjoyed reading your piece or I would not have been annoyed at mislaying it.

   At any rate, I don't know whether I can keep it or not, so I'm returning the manuscript to you. When it is printed in *Chicago Review,* would you ask them to send me a copy?

And for now, my best to you,
Norman Mailer

TO: ROGER SHATTUCK

Mailer met Roger Shattuck, the art critic, in Brooklyn in the 1950s. The Village Voice *review appeared on 13 May 1965. The three novels named in the first paragraph, were written by, respectively, Joseph Heller (1923-2000), James T. Farrell (1904-1979) and Ernest Hemingway (1899-1961). Mailer and his daughter Susan translated and published "Lament for Ignacio Sanchez Mejias" by Federico Garcia Lorca (1898-*

1936) in The Poetry Bag *(winter 1967-68). Stephen Spender (1909-1995), the poet, was editor of the British publication* Queen Magazine *in the early 1960s. He published some of Mailer's poems there in April 1962. Johann Wolfgang von Goethe (1749-1832), the German man of letters, is greatly admired by Mailer. The novel Mailer mentions "getting started on" at the end of the second paragraph is the "big book" he had been trying to write since 1959. He mentions it in several subsequent letters, but it was abandoned later in the summer when he shifted to work on a stage version of* The Deer Park.

142 Columbia Heights
Brooklyn 1, New York
June 8, 1965

Dear Roger,

I didn't mind the review in the *Village Voice*—I naturally thought it was unduly critical, but since I have two attitudes about the novel, thinking on some days that it's a marvelous piece of crap and on others that it's the only thing new anybody has done since god knows when, since *Catch-22* [1961] or *Studs Lonigan* [1935], or Christ, since *The Sun Also Rises* [1926]. I read reviews with interest now, looking for a clue. Anyway, yours was interesting.

The idea of the translations intrigues me, but I don't know yet where or if I would fit. My best language by far is French, only I've no desire to translate anything in that language since my French is not nearly good enough. I've a smattering of Spanish [and], would like to translate Garcia Lorca's "Lament for Ignacio Sanchez Mejias." I read a translation [Stephen] Spender made of that poem once and knew after going through twenty lines that I could do better with my left hand. Still, that isn't really my heart's desire, in fact I don't know that yet. I suspect I'd rather try translating something in a language I know hardly at all. Some early [Johann Wolfgang von] Goethe, or some Latin or Greek. At any rate, Roger, let me think about this for a period, and remind me about this in six months perhaps. You see, right now I'm getting started on another novel, and so certainly don't want to get into any of this.

Last thought. A guy named Bud Shrake is planning to open a bookstore in Austin, and got a half promise from me to go down for the opening. Perhaps we could work something up with the kids at the same time. Only for four or five days on a campus is not my idea of heaven, since all the college kids I know or have ever met seem to do nothing but ask questions, nine-tenths of them the sort which can be answered by IBM cards, and I always feel like a decrepit machine with burned-out fuses by the time I get away. It's one thing to live with these kids all year, every year, that I imagine can be just as good as anything else, but, Roger, I don't know if you have any idea of what it's like to take them on for twenty-four hours, or seventy-two. No matter, it looks as if we'll have something to discuss in the fall. Right now I'm off to Provincetown for four months of good work, I hope.

Give my best to Nora,
Norman

TO: DIANA TRILLING

142 Columbia Heights
Brooklyn 1, New York
June 8, 1965

Dear Diana,

Just a line. I'm getting ready to start work on a novel, so I'm doing my best to try to clear up correspondence ruthlessly, ruthlessly. There's no pleasure in it now, but the alternative is to let it feed upon half the week. But it does deprive me of writing a long letter in answer to yours, and that's a shame because I think in replying to your honest and most gently stated criticisms of *An American Dream* I would have formulated certain things about the book for myself. I don't know if I'm getting mellow or if it's the nature of the book itself, or even just the way the book was written, but for the first time I've written a novel about which I feel altogether two-headed, which is that there are any number of occasions when my private opinion comes close to the worst of the reviewers, and I really think it is an extraordinary piece of crap. But of course there are just as many other days when I decide quite calmly that it's probably the first novel to come along since *The Sun Also Rises* which has anything really new in it. And that with all my faults, I'm the only one around who's doing anything interesting in writing at all. So you can see that with this unresolved argument going on in my dear head I hardly can get excited when my friends are unhappy about the whole thing. Anyway, angel, you and Lionel will be back in the fall. Maybe by then it will be clearer in all our heads. Incidentally, we're going to be in Provincetown until October 5. So if you come to the city before then and it inspires you with horror, which has happened to me after many a year in Europe, and you feel that you have to get out for a few days, take a flying trip up to us. We're going to have lots of room this summer and would of course love to have all two of you, all three of you, however it might go.

Give our best to Guronay and Margie, and the very best of everything to Lionel,

Norman

P.S. I look forward to your description of Upton House up close, and bless you for your jealousy when they said nice things. How human you are. The very last one.

Norman

TO: JOHN A. MEIXNER

Meixner was a writer friend. The Saul Bellow (1915-) novel Mailer
refers to is Herzog *(1964).*

142 Columbia Heights
Brooklyn 1, New York
June 12, 1965

Dear John,

Thank you for your letter, I read it over several times with interest,
and I'm afraid I agree with much of what you said, maybe most of it.
This is a dreadful thing to say, and I know that I should never compare
myself with other swords, but if I had known last year that the best
thing in Bellow's next novel was going to be that his professor was
really and truly a professor in the details of his mind, then maybe I
would have taken a little more trouble with mine, or had the sense to
make him a *Life* photographer. The main fault with the goddamn book
I think is that I was saying to the reader, "Look, you know I can create
a professor and I can give him intimate insides of his mind, I just don't
want to be bothered with that. I'm too busy to go through the three or
four or five months of reading, and you're all too lazy, now admit it, to
have your heads stuffed. So let's just accept the fact that the man's a
professor, call it a convention, and let it go at that." But of course no
one did. And now I have to wonder myself. Perhaps it was a mistake to
do it the way I did it. Perhaps I should have reworked the book, but
then if I had, the pace would have been lost. And I am guilty of having
liked the pace of the book. Maybe all of this is what happens when you
write in installments.

Anyway, I'm off now for the summer to start work on a new novel.
Let us see if this is the big objective one. You are, by the way, so far as I
know, the first one to point out this alternation. I thought I was the
only one who was on to that.

A good summer to you,
Norman

TO: DIANA TRILLING

The "Marlow" Trilling refers to is the narrator-participant used by
Joseph Conrad (1857-1924) in several fictional works he wrote based on
his seafaring experiences: "Youth" (1898), Lord Jim *(1900),* Heart of
Darkness *(1902), and "Chance" (1912). Mabel Dodge Luhan (1879-*
1962) was a supporter of D.H. Lawrence (1885-1930) when he lived in
New Mexico.

607 Commercial Street
Provincetown, Massachusetts
July 14, 1965

80

Dear Diana,

Thank you for the clipping and the nice reports. I'm not sure I know what you mean by the absence of a Marlow in *An American Dream*. Superficially it seems to me that Rojack embodies a sufficient amount of civilization to avoid meaninglessness, but to defend that in detail means a long letter, and then we shall both be breaking our vows to write many pages this summer and few letters. Therefore I save the discussion for the pleasure of seeing you and Lionel in September. By the way, our place is on the sea and most agreeable. I hope you and Lionel (and Jim if he's so inclined) are in the mood to come here when you get back.

Love,

Norman

P.S. There's a somewhat unintegrated book by a man named Christopher Lasch, called if I remember *The New Radicalism in America,* but it has a very good chapter on Mabel Dodge Luhan in which [D.H.] Lawrence figures prominently, and I think you might enjoy it.

TO: JOHN W. ALDRIDGE

607 Commercial Street

Provincetown, Massachusetts

August 17, 1965

Dear Jack,

It's too bad we missed each other this summer, it really is. I was looking forward to it. I've been working hard too, and kept putting off a letter until a weekend would show on the horizon that looked to be good. So it went by. We were thinking last spring of going to Nantucket in a boat that a friend of ours had in Harwichport, but he chose to go to Hawaii, so that took care of that.

The re-reprinting of your review in *Partisan* [Review] also did not take place. Phillips said that he would do it, but also asked me if I really thought it would be effective after all this time, and all the extra emphasis that it demanded, and I had to agree with him. It would have made me look silly, and worse, in this sort of small matter, might have made you look bad. Which after all was not my purpose. As you may remember, my agent approached Warner's. As I feared, they have not answered yes or no, which in Hollywood always means no. The difficulty from the beginning is that movie companies do not get technical advisors in order to make the author's meaning clear to them. They look for technical advisors who keep them running well in the middle of the prejudices of the particular consensus against which the work was aimed. Thus if they were to make a movie today of *The Naked and the Dead,* the technical advisor would be a man from the Pentagon; so the technical advisor of *An American Dream,* if there will be one, is bound to prove out a retired commissioner of police from the City of New York.

Well, now we must look forward to seeing each other in the fall.

Best and all,
Norman

TO: IRVING J. WEISS

A literary host at a radio station in New York, Weiss sought Mailer's involvement in a couple of literary projects.

607 Commercial Street
Provincetown, Massachusetts
August 26, 1965

Dear Mr. Weiss,

By the time your letter was forwarded, it was August 19. But then in any case I couldn't have heard your reading of [Malcolm] de Chazal, since I've been up here in Provincetown trying to work on a novel, and don't get WBAI as far as I know. At any rate, this gives me an opportunity to thank you for your letter, because it's the first to come from somebody who did not like *An American Dream* at first and then went through the odd barrier of the book to like it. Most people seemed either to like it very much or to dislike it very much, and make that the end of it.

Also, this is to ask you when and where your translation of Sens-Plastique will appear.

Yours sincerely,
Norman Mailer

TO: LIONEL ABEL

Abel (1911-2001) was a drama professor and critic who wrote for Partisan Review *and moved in the same leftist intellectual circles as Mailer. Abel referred to Mailer in a* Partisan Review *essay as "Mindbad the Mailer." Mailer was on the Board of the leftist journal* Dissent *with Stanley Plastrick, Emanuel Geltman and Irving Howe (1920-1973), who was its editor.* An American Tragedy *(1925) was written by Theodore Dreiser (1871-1945), one of Mailer's literary heroes. He saw* An American Dream *an extension of Dreiser's novel and very consciously chose his title to echo it.*

142 Columbia Heights
Brooklyn 1, New York
February 28, 1966

Dear Lionel,

Yes, it is possible my mind has gone somewhat bad over the years. Yet, in consolation, my memory for titles remains intact. *The American Dream,* as you call it, seems actually to be *An American Dream.* (I was thinking you see of *An American Tragedy.*) But, if you cannot read even the first word of my book, then it occurs to me your brain if still ready, is either unwilling or unable, dear Lionel —

Yours,
Mindbad Mailer

cc: Irving Howe
     Stanley Plastrick
     Emanuel Geltman

TO: MANN RUBIN

Rubin wrote the first screenplay for An American Dream, *one that was altered considerably by Warner Brothers. For example, the setting was changed to Los Angeles. Janet Leigh did indeed play Cherry.*

142 Columbia Heights
Brooklyn 1, New York
March 24, 1966

Dear Mann Rubin,

Well, your letter confirmed the little messages I was getting in my dreams, and so I got to work on my agent, who's gotten to work on Warner's, and that of course accomplished wonders, you bet. Now I hear they've got Janet Leigh playing Cherry. Someday they will do the life of Jennie Grossinger, and Tuesday Weld will sit on Natalie Wood's head long enough to grind the kasha in the second reel. Well, Mann, when you come to New York, give me a ring and we will commiserate — UL 58966.

Yours in show biz,
Norman Mailer

TO: LONNIE L. WELLS

Wells was a Mailer fan. The use of historical characters in novels did not originate with Mailer, of course, but the practice became more common after An American Dream. *For example, E.L. Doctorow (1931-), who worked on Mailer's novel as a young editor at* Dial, *depicted Harry Houdini, Henry Ford, J.P. Morgan and several other historical figures in his 1975 nonfiction novel,* Ragtime. *It appears that Mailer was the first to use J.F.K. in a novel. He used Kennedy again as a character in his 1991 CIA novel,* Harlot's Ghost.

> 142 Columbia Heights
> Brooklyn 1, New York
> April 16, 1966

Dear Lonnie Wells,

I'm afraid I can't answer your question definitively. I don't know of any other work of fiction where John Kennedy appears as a character on or off the immediate scene of the novel. But of course, that is not at all the same thing as knowing that *An American Dream* is certainly the first book of that sort.

> Yours sincerely,
> Norman Mailer

TO: SUSAN ABRAMS

In this letter to fan Susan Abrams, Mailer is referring to the film version of the novel. Friends told him it was awful.

> 565 Commercial Street
> Provincetown, Massachusetts
> September 24, 1966

Dear Susan,

Just a line to say hello. *An American Dream* is awful. No excuses I'm afraid, I just sold it. As for the recommendation, of course I knew.

> Best, etc.,
> Norman Mailer

TO: YALE M. UDOFF

Udoff was acquainted with both Mailer and Mann Rubin.

> 565 Commercial Street
> Provincetown, Massachusetts
> September 24, 1966

Dear Yale,

Thanks for your letter. Tell Mann Rubin I'd like to see his original screenplay of An American Dream in order to get a better idea of how and where Warner's fucked it.

> Best, etc.
> Norman

TO: NANCY WEBER

Weber's interview with Mailer appeared in the March 1965 issue of
Books, *the literary supplement of the* New York Post. *It is one of only a
few interviews he gave on the novel before it was published. Mailer did
not know anything at the time about how Warner Brothers intended to
film the novel and speculated in the interview on whether Frank Sinatra
could play Stephen Rojack. He also discussed the possibility of making*
An American Dream *the first volume of a quartet in the manner of* The
Alexandria Quartet *(1957-1960) of Lawrence Durrell (1912-1990), and
commented on how* An American Dream *had its roots in his November
1960* Esquire *essay on J.F.K., "Superman Comes to the Supermarket."
On the advice of friends, Mailer has never seen the film version of the
novel.* The Deer Park *was turned into a play by Mailer and ran from 31
January to 21 May 1967 at the Off-Broadway Theatre de Lys.*

> 565 Commercial Street
> Provincetown, Massachusetts
> September 24, 1966

Dear Nancy,

I'm sorry to take so long to answer, but I haven't gone near my mail
in two months, and now I'm hacking my way through. It's the only way
to stay alive. As for the film *An American Dream,* I haven't seen it, but
then I hardly suppose you have to. The only thing is, I wouldn't do an
interview because I think if you sell something to Hollywood you're one
of the whores in the deal, and a whore shouldn't complain about other
whores, for that's the basis of all comedy, so we'll leave it at that.

I'll be back in New York in November, and a few of us are going to
produce *The Deer Park* Off-Broadway. We were doing it up here this
summer. Maybe we can do an interview then.

Incidentally, although I think it can't be easy on you, I'm glad you're
off the *Post.* You're much too skillful an interviewer, let alone a writer,
to work for that "schlockeria."

> Love and all,
> Norman

TO: LOUIS and MOOS MAILER

The first stage version of The Deer Park, *in two acts, was presented at Act
IV, a Provincetown Theater, in August 1966, with Beverly Bentley as Lulu
Myers.* Cannibals and Christians, *Mailer's third miscellany, was
published by Dial on 29 August 1966. Beverly gave birth to Stephen
McLeod Mailer, their second son, on 10 March 1966. Basil was the son
of Louis and Moos.*

565 Commercial Street
Provincetown, Massachusetts
September 25, 1966

Dear Louis and Moos,

I haven't written in ages. Please forgive me for not answering your fine letters, but this summer's been unbelievable. I haven't worked so hard in years. I got going at a great rate on a new novel and then just about the time I was half way through, everything in the scheme of things diverted me over to an old adaptation of *The Deer Park,* which I rewrote and changed from a five-hour play to a two-hour play. We did it up here in Provincetown in a theater Beverly helped to start (she is, by the way, a superb actress—woe is me—I'm not used to other talent in the family), and the play turned out well enough to be moved to New York. So we're going to put it in on Off-Broadway this winter and if all goes well, it might be exciting, indeed. I have some hopes at any rate. As for the rest, all is well. Mother's recovered completely from the operation, which proved, of course, not to be necessary—when will people finally realize that medicine exists first for the sake of doctors and their beastly hospitals. *Cannibals and Christians* came out and, to my surprise, received fairly good reviews. If Dad hasn't taken care of it, I'm going to make certain a copy gets to you.

As for the boys, Michael is all box-office, prima donna, narcissistic, brilliant, spoiled, electric, frighteningly sexy, a complete self-starter, and Steve all attention and reaction and soft smiles and chuckles and fun. They're going to make a great pair, knock on wood, as my mother would say.

As for the movie, *An American Dream,* don't ask. An absolute disaster. My only consolation is that I had nothing to do with the makings of it, except for the tarty action of taking a large sum of money in sale from a large movie studio, for which I had no respect.

Give my best to Basil. Beverly sends love.

Norman

TO: SANFORD STERNLICHT

Sanford Sternlicht, an English professor at New York State University College at Oswego, wanted Mailer's opinion of the film version.

565 Commercial Street
Provincetown, Massachusetts
September 26, 1966

Dear Sandy,

Just a line to tell you that we may be in Provincetown Christmas week, for we own a home here now, but if we're in New York, we'll look forward to seeing you. You write, "We have as not yet seen *An Ameri-*

can Dream and find it difficult to imagine it confined to the screen." Yes indeed, Sir, when you see it, you may find it difficult to imagine.

Best,

Norman

TO: WHIT BURNETT

Mailer's story "The Greatest Thing in the World" won Story *magazine's national college contest and was published there by Burnett in November 1941, marking the beginning of Mailer's literary career. His undated letter (probably written in 1969) prefaces a selection from* An American Dream *describing the murder of Deborah by Rojack that was published in Burnett's 1970 anthology,* This Is My Best: In the Third Quarter of the Century. *Mailer's letter is perhaps his most considered and perceptive comment on the novel.*

Dear Whit,

Sometimes it seems useful to think of two kinds of novels—novels of manners, and modern explosive surrealistic novels in which the very notion of society, let alone manners, is bulldozed away in order to see what strange skeletons of fish and what buried treasure comes up in the ore. Out of my own work I suppose *Why Are We in Vietnam?* would most satisfy the latter category, and *An American Dream* might prove for some to be my most substantial attack on the problem of writing a novel of manners. They are hard novels to do well. Now that we are approaching the end of the seventh decade of the twentieth century they are becoming novels which are almost impossible to do well. The old totemistic force of manners, the old totemistic belief that breaching a manner inspired a curse has been all but lost in the avalanche of social deterioration which characterizes our era. Yet what can appear more attractive and sinister to us than a tea ceremony at the edge of a cliff. So I often think *An American Dream* is my best book. I tried for more in this novel than anywhere else and hence was living for a while with themes not easily accessible to literary criticism, not even to examination. The passage I choose now is not obligatorily the best thousand words in the work, but comes from the latter part of the first chapter and therefore offers few discomforts of orientation to the reader, and no demand on me for a synopsis of preceding events. Perhaps it may also serve to illumine the fine nerve of dread back of every good manner. Manner is the mandarin of mood, and in the shattering of every mood is an existential breath—does laughter or the murderous next ensue?

Yours,

Norman Mailer

Illustrations

Back panel of dust wrapper of the Dial press edition: photograph of
Mailer by Anne Barry

Have you been following Norman Mailer's installment
novel in ESQUIRE? Dial Press has signed up to publish
it in hard-cover, Dell in paperback, Warner Brothers to
make a movie. And it isn't even finished.

Advertisement in the *New York Times* for the *Esquire* serial version,
22 April 1964.

An American Dream A New Novel Serialized Exclusively in Esquire by Norman Mailer Installment One: The Harbors of the Moon

Norman Mailer

EVERY one of you finds yourself lonely, but you discover your loneliness by living a life which is like the life of everyone else; you are understood perfectly: it is just that nobody wants to listen. Still, you hear of men and women who have a life which proves to be their own; history records their name because they found no place. Ernest Hemingway is the first who comes to mind, and Marilyn Monroe. So too does Patterson, Floyd Patterson, and Liston; Edith Piaf and Dr. Stephen Ward; Christine Jorgensen, Porfirio Rubirosa, Luis Miguel Dominguín. So too do I—to myself at least. For I take from this second species of loneliness a property which is peculiar to us: we believe in coincidences and take our memory from meetings. I know I measure my life by such a rule. I met Jack Kennedy, for instance, in 1946. We were both war heroes and were both Freshmen in Congress. Congressman John Fitzgerald Kennedy, Democrat from Massachusetts, and Congressman Stephen Richards Rojack, Democrat from New York. We even spent part of one night together on a long double date and it promised to be a good night for me. I stole his girl.

Title and opening paragraph of the first installment of *An American Dream* in *Esquire*, January 1964

93

2 CHAPTER

Green Circles of Exhaustion

Well, if Deborah's dying had given me a new life, I must be all of eight hours old by now, I had lived through a night, I had come into a morning. It was morning outside on the street; I could think of the sun coming up. But it rose into a wintry smog, a wet wan morning grey with mist, the sun glowed feebly on my mind while I drank the dark burnished midnight in this Miami club transported to New York, this after-hours box of leatherette, flame-orange stuffing for the booths, the stools, the face of the bar, black carpet, purple wine ceiling, recessed spots just so gloomy as the reading lights above an airplane seat, and so sated as the lights of a harem—I was thus proud in the fevers of fatigue that my bourbon on the rocks revolved a majestic route down through my chest, the congestions of my lungs, the maze of my belly, those peppered links in my gut. The police were gone and would be back again tomorrow; the newspapers were already being dropped at the early morning stands; in a few hours the details of my daily life would erupt like a house gone mad with the electric dishwasher screaming at the delivery boy, the television studio would be on the phone, and I might have to be on the phone to the university, Deborah's friends would call, there would be the funeral, God, the funeral, the funeral, and the first in a new thousand to twenty-two thousand lies. But I was like a wrecked mariner in the lull between two storms. No better indeed I was close to a strong old man dying now of his overwork, passing into death by way of going deeper to himself. Rich mahoganies of color move in to support his heart and there are tired angels to meet him after work, a rich

First page of chapter four of the novel (misidentified as chapter two) in *Dial Souvenir Sampler / 1964.*

Cover of *Publishers' Weekly* featuring the forthcoming Dial Press
version of *An American Dream*, 12 October 1964.

THE BOOKSELLER DECEMBER 26, 1964   DECEMBER BOOK LIST

THE BOOKSELLER

THE ORGAN OF THE BOOK TRADE

No. 3079   (Regd. at the G.P.O. as a Newspaper.)   SATURDAY, DECEMBER 26, 1964   Price 1s 3d

NORMAN MAILER

an american dream

ANDRE DEUTSCH   MARCH   21/-

Cover of the British trade journal, *The Bookseller,* 26 December 1964,
featuring the forthcoming British edition of *An American Dream,*
published by Andre Deutsch.

UNCORRECTED PROOFS

AN
AMERICAN
DREAM

by Norman Mailer

The Dial Press   *Nineteen Sixty-Five*   New York

Cover of uncorrected page proof of the Dial Press edition.

Front and spine of dust wrapper of the Dial Press edition.

Invitation to the reception for the novel at the Village Vanguard in New York on publication day, 15 March 1965.

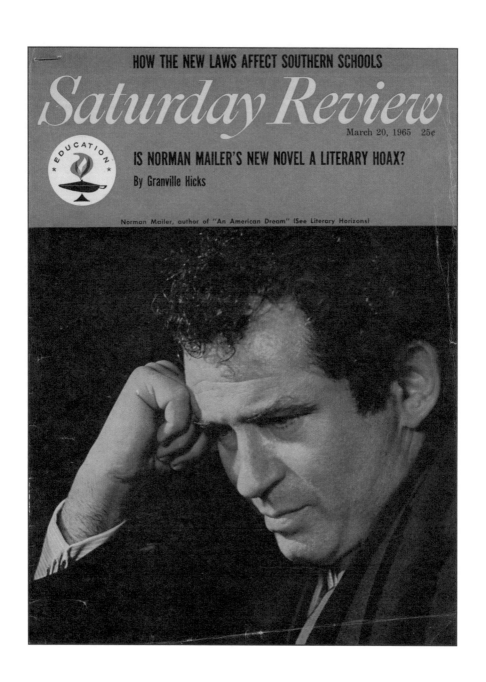

Cover of 20 March 1965 *Saturday Review* depicting Mailer

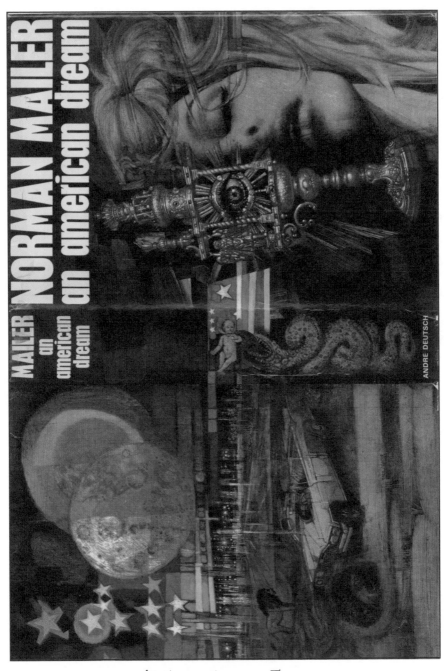

Dust wrapper of the British edition of *An American Dream* published by Andre Deutsch on 26 April 1965

The list below, based on reports received from leading booksellers around the nation (see below for stores reporting this week), is meant to indicate which books are currently the most popular in the U. S.—not which are the best. Books deemed by Book Week critics to be of special literary, social or historic interest are marked thus (✳)—The Editors.

Week's Score	*FICTION*	*Weeks Listed*
1✳	**The Ambassador, by Morris L. West** A novel about a U. S. diplomat in South Viet Nam.	5
2✳	**Up the Down Staircase, by Bel Kaufman** Inside a New York City public school.	11
3	**Hotel, by Arthur Hailey** Behind the scenes at a luxury hotel in the South.	9
4	**Don't Stop the Carnival, by Herman Wouk** The Caribbean adventures of a Broadway press agent.	9
5✳	**Herzog, by Saul Bellow** A middle-aged intellectual searches for peace of mind.	32
6	**The Flight of the Falcon, by Daphne du Maurier** A murder in Rome leads to a search of the past.	3
7	**A Pillar of Iron, by Taylor Caldwell** An historical novel about Cicero and Caesar.	2
8✳	**Hurry Sundown, by K. B. Gilden** A Negro and a white farmer in Georgia struggle to keep their land.	15
9	**Funeral in Berlin, by Len Deighton** A Cold War spy story.	15
10✳	**An American Dream, by Norman Mailer** The mythic portrayal of an American hero.	7

Bestseller list in *Book Week,* 30 May 1965,
showing the novel in No. 10 position.

102

Advertisement for film version of the novel
from Warner Brothers Pressbook.

DELL
0129
1.50

An American Dream / Norman Mailer

Cover of third Dell paperback edition, published February 1970.

Appendix I
Norman Mailer: Key Publications, 1948-2003

The Naked and the Dead (1948) Novel
Barbary Shore (1951) Novel
The Deer Park (1955) Novel
Advertisements for Myself (1959) Miscellany
Deaths for the Ladies (and Other Disasters) (1962) Poems
The Presidential Papers (1963) Miscellany
An American Dream (1965) Novel
Cannibals and Christians (1966) Miscellany
The Short Fiction of Norman Mailer (1967)
The Deer Park: A Play (1967)
Why Are We in Vietnam? (1967) Novel
The Armies of the Night (1968) Nonfiction Narrative
Miami and the Siege of Chicago (1968) Nonfiction Narrative
Of a Fire on the Moon (1971) Nonfiction Narrative
The Prisoner of Sex (1971) Essay
The Long Patrol: 25 Years of Writing from the Work of Norman Mailer,
    ed. Robert F. Lucid (1971) Selections from 13 of Mailer's works
Existential Errands (1972) Miscellany
St. George and the Godfather (1972) Nonfiction Narrative
Marilyn: A Biography (1973)
The Fight (1975) Nonfiction Narrative
Genius and Lust: A Journey through the Major Writings of Henry Miller,
    ed. Norman Mailer (1976) Includes 80 pages of Mailer's commentary
A Transit to Narcissus (1978) Novel
The Executioner's Song (1979) Nonfiction Narrative
Of Women and Their Elegance (1980) Novel
Pieces and Pontifications (1982) Essays and Interviews; Interviews,
    ed. J. Michael Lennon
Ancient Evenings (1983) Novel
Tough Guys Don't Dance (1984) Novel
Conversations with Norman Mailer, ed. J. Michael Lennon (1988)
Harlot's Ghost (1991) Novel
Oswald's Tale (1995) Biography
Portrait of Picasso as a Young Man: An Interpretive Biography (1995)
The Gospel according to the Son (1997) Novel
The Time of Our Time (1998) Retrospective Anthology
The Spooky Art: Some Thoughts on Writing,
    ed. J. Michael Lennon (2003) Miscellany
Why Are We at War? (2003) Essay
Modest Gifts: Poems and Drawings (2003)

Appendix II
An American Dream:
Selected Bibliography

Critical Studies

Adams, Laura. *Existential Battles: The Growth of Norman Mailer.* Athens: Ohio University Press, 1976.

_____, editor. *Will the Real Norman Mailer Please Stand Up.* Port Washington, N.Y.: Kennikat Press, 1974.

Aldridge, John W. *Time to Murder and Create: The Contemporary Novel in Crisis.* New York: David McKay, 1966.

Begiebing, Robert. *Acts of Regeneration: Allegory and Archetype in the Work of Norman Mailer.* Columbia: University of Missouri Press, 1980.

Bloom, Harold, editor. *Norman Mailer: Modern Critical Views.* New York: Chelsea House, 1986.

Braudy, Leo, editor. *Norman Mailer: A Collection of Critical Essays.* Englewood Cliffs, N. J.: Prentice-Hall, 1972.

Bufithis, Philip M. *Norman Mailer.* New York: Ungar, 1978.

Cotkin, George. *Existential America.* Baltimore: Johns Hopkins University Press, 2003.

Dickstein, Morris. *Leopards in the Temple: The Transformation of American Fiction, 1945-1970.* Cambridge: Harvard University Press, 2002.

Ehrlich, Robert. *Norman Mailer: The Radical as Hipster.* Metuchen, N.J: Scarecrow Press, 1978.

Fetterly, Judith. *The Resisting Reader: A Feminist Approach to American Fiction.* Bloomington: Indiana University Press, 1978.

Glenday, Michael K. *Norman Mailer.* New York: St. Martin's Press, 1995.

Glickman, Susan. "The World as Will and Idea: A Comparative Study of *An American Dream* and *Mr. Sammler's Planet." Modern Fiction Studies* 28 (winter 1982-83), 569-82.

Gordon, Andrew. *An American Dreamer: A Psychological Study of the Fiction of Norman Mailer.* Cranbury, N.J.: Associated University Presses, 1980.

Gutman, Stanley T. *Mankind in Barbary: The Individual and Society in the Novels of Norman Mailer.* Hanover, N.H.: University Press of New England, 1975.

Kaufmann, Donald L. *Norman Mailer: The Countdown (The First Twenty Years).* Carbondale: Southern Illinois University Press, 1969.

Langbaum, Robert. *The Modern Spirit: Essays on the Continuity of Nineteenth and Twentieth Century Literature.* New York: Oxford University Press, 1970.

Leeds, Barry H. *The Structured Vision of Norman Mailer.* New York University Press, 1969.

_____. *The Enduring Vision of Norman Mailer.* Bainbridge Island, Wash.: Pleasure Boat Studio, 2003.

Lennon, J. Michael, editor. *Critical Essays on Norman Mailer.* Boston: G.K. Hall, 1986.

Lucid, Robert F. *Norman Mailer: The Man and His Work.* Boston: Little, Brown, 1971.

Madden, David, editor. *American Dreams, American Nightmares.* Southern Illinois University Press, 1970.

McConnell, Frank D. *Four Postwar American Novelists: Bellow, Mailer, Barth and Pynchon.* Chicago: University of Chicago Press, 1977.

Merrill, Robert. *Norman Mailer Revisited.* Boston: Twayne, 1992.

Parker, Hershel. *Flawed Texts and Verbal Icons: Literary Authority in American Fiction.* Evanston, Ill.: Northwestern University, Press,1984.

Poirier, Richard. *Norman Mailer.* New York: Viking, 1972.

Radford, Jean. *Norman Mailer: A Critical Study.* New York: Harper and Row, 1975.

Schulz, Max F. *Radical Sophistication: Studies in Contemporary Jewish-American Novelists.* Athens: Ohio University Press, 1969.

Solotaroff, Robert. *Down Mailer's Way.* Urbana: University of Illinois Press, 1974.

Tanner, Tony. *City of Words: American Fiction, 1950-1970.* New York: Harper and Row, 1971.

Toback, James. "Norman Mailer Today." *Commentary,* October 1967, 67-76.

Wagenheim, Allan J. "Square's Progress: *An American Dream.*" *Critique* 10 (1968), 45-68.

Wood, Margery. "Norman Mailer and Nathalie Sarraute: A Comparison of Existential Novels." *Minnesota Review* 6 (1966), 68-76.

Weinberg, Helen A. *The New Novel in America: The Kafkan Mode in Contemporary Fiction.* New York: Cornell University Press, 1970.

Interviews

Adams, Laura. "Existential Aesthetics: An Interview with Norman Mailer." *Partisan Review* 42 (summer 1975), 197-214. Reprinted in *Conversations with Norman Mailer*, edited by J. Michael Lennon. Jackson: University Press of Mississippi, 1988.

Brower, Brock. "In this Corner, Norman Mailer: Never the Champion, Always the Challenger." *Life*, 15 October 1965, 94-96, 98, 100, 102, 105-6, 109-12,115, 117.

Carroll, Paul. "Playboy Interview: Norman Mailer." *Playboy,* January 1968, 69-72, 74, 76, 78, 80, 82-84. Reprinted in Lucid.

Gelmis, Joseph. "Norman Mailer." *The Film Director as Superstar.* New York: Doubleday, 1970.

Matz, Charles. "Mailer's Opera." *Opera News,* 21 February 1970, 14-16.

"Mr. Mailer Interviews Himself." *New York Times Book Review*, 17 September 1967, 4-5, 40. Reprinted in *Conversations with Norman Mailer.*

Medwick, Cathleen. "Norman Mailer on Love, Sex, God and the Devil." *Vogue*, December 1980, 268-69, 322. Partially reprinted in Mailer's *Pieces and Pontifications.* Boston: Little, Brown, 1982.

"Norman Mailer on *An American Dream.*" Interview with unidentified interviewer. *New York Post*, 25 March 1965, 38. Reprinted in *Conversations with Norman Mailer.*

Weber, Nancy. "Norman Mailer's 'American Dream': Superman Returns." *Books, New York Post,* March 1965, 14-16.

Young, Gavin. "A Conversation with Norman Mailer." *Observer Weekly* (London), 26 April 1964, 26.

Reviews

Aldridge, John W. "The Big Comeback of Norman Mailer." *Life*, 19 March 1965, 12. Reprinted in expanded form in Aldridge and Braudy.

Alvarez, A. "Norman X." *Spectator,* 7 May 1965, 603.

Bersani, Leo. "The Interpretation of Dreams." *Partisan Review* 32 (fall 1965), 603-8. Reprinted in Braudy and Lucid.

Corrington, John William. "An American Dreamer." *Chicago Review* 18 (1965), 58-66.

Didion, Joan "A Social Eye." *National Review,* 20 April 1965, 329-30.

Epstein, Joseph. "Norman X: The Literary Man's Cassius Clay." *New Republic,* 17 April 1965, 22-25.

Hardwick, Elizabeth. "Bad Boy." *Partisan Review* 32 (spring 1965), 291-94. Reprinted in Lucid.

Hicks, Granville. "A Literary Hoax." *Saturday Review,* 20 March 1965, 23-24.

Hyman, Stanley E. "Norman Mailer's Yummy Rump." *New Leader*, 15 March 1965, 16-17. Reprinted in Braudy.

"In Carcinoma City." *Times* (London) *Literary Supplement*, 29 April 1965, 325.

Kermode, Frank. "Rammel," *New Statesman*, 14 May 1965, 765-66.

Knickerbocker, Conrad. "A Man Desperate for a New Life." *New York Times Book Review,* 14 March 1965, 1, 36, 38-39.

Muste, John M. "Nightmarish Mailer." *Progressive*, February 1965, 49-51.

Pickrel, Paul. "Thing of Darkness." *Harper's*, April 1965, 116-17.

Poirier, Richard. " 'Morbid-Mindedness'." *Commentary*, June 1965, 91-94. Reprinted in Lucid.

Rahv, Philip. "Crime without Punishment." *New York Review of Books*, 25 March 1965, 1-4.

Ricks, Christopher. "Saint Stephen." *New Statesman,* 30 April 1965, 687.

Shattuck, Roger. "Books: *An American Dream.*" *Village Voice,* 13 May 1965, 5, 22.

Weber, Brom. "A Fear of Dying: Norman Mailer's *An American Dream.*" *Hollins Critic,* 2 (June 1965), 8-11.

Wolfe, Tom. "Son of Crime and Punishment; Or, How to Go Eight Rounds with the Heavyweight Champ—and Lose." *Book Week (New York Herald Tribune)*, 14 March 1965, 1, 10, 12-13. Reprinted in Lucid.

Appendix III
Timeline of Events, 1962-1966

Most of the events listed below are discussed or mentioned in the 76 letters in this edition; several additional events have been included to give a sense of the milestones and upheavals in Mailer's life and the life of the nation during this period.

1962

30 January: NM's first volume of poems, *Deaths for the Ladies (and Other Disasters),* is published by Putnam's

Late March: NM divorces his second wife, Adele Morales, in Juarez, Mexico.

April: NM marries Lady Jean Campbell and they move into his apartment at 142 Columbia Heights in Brooklyn.

Mid-August: NM submits the first (of 14) columns, titled "The Big Bite," for publication in the November *Esquire.*

18 August: NM's third daughter, Kate, born to Jean Campbell.

22 September: NM debates William F. Buckley, Jr. on "The Role of the Right Wing" before an audience of 4,000 in Chicago.

25 September: NM covers the first heavyweight prizefight between Floyd Patterson and Sonny Liston in Chicago.

October-November: Cuban Missile Crisis. The Soviet Union removes missile sites from Cuba after the U.S. threatens a military attack.

Late fall: NM separates from Jean Campbell.

December: NM publishes the first of six columns of reflections on Martin Buber's *Tales of the Hasidim* in *Commentary.*

20 December: "An Open Letter to JFK from Norman Mailer" appears in the *Village Voice.*

January-February: *Playboy* publishes in two parts the NM-Buckley debate.

February: "Ten Thousand Words a Minute," NM's account of the first Patterson-Liston fight in September 1963, is published in *Esquire*.

1963

March: NM meets Beverly Bentley.

24 March: NM speaks on existentialism and psychoanalysis at Harvard.

31 May: NM presents "An Existential Evening" at Carnegie Hall, discussing the FBI, President Kennedy and Communism with the audience.

Summer: "The First Presidential Paper," NM's essay on heroes and leaders, is published in *Dissent*.

July-August: NM and Beverly drive cross-country and back, stopping in Arkansas, Las Vegas (where they see the second Patterson-Liston fight with Liston again the winner), San Francisco and Georgia.

28 August: Martin Luther King, Jr. delivers his "I Have a Dream" speech at the Washington Monument during the Civil Rights March on the Capital.

Late Summer: Scott Meredith becomes NM's literary agent and helps broker the sale of an unwritten novel to Dial Press and Dell Books. NM proposes and *Esquire* editor Harold Hayes agrees to the serial publication of this novel in the magazine, January through August 1964.

29 September: NM's review of Victor Lasky's *J.F.K.: The Man and the Myth* appears in *Book Week (N.Y. Herald Tribune)*.

Mid-October: NM turns in the first of eight installments of the novel to *Esquire*.

8 November: Putnam's publishes *The Presidential Papers,* a collection of assorted prose focused on J.F.K.

Mid-November: The December *Esquire* containing NM's final "Big Bite" column is published. NM announces in it that he will write a novel called *An American Dream,* in eight installments, beginning in the January 1964 issue. He completes the second installment at about the same time.

16 November: Shortly after obtaining a Mexican divorce from Jean Campbell, Mailer marries Beverly Bentley

22 November: President Kennedy is assassinated in Dallas. Vice President Johnson is sworn in as President.

27 November: NM begins working on the third installment.

Mid-December: The January issue of *Esquire* containing the first installment appears.

26 December: NM contributes to a *New York Review of Books* symposium on J.F.K. His 175-word contribution is echoed in his "Special Preface to the Bantam Edition" of *The Presidential Papers* published in May 1964.

1964

Mid-January: The fourth installment of the novel is completed.

Late January: NM debates William F. Buckley, Jr. in New York on a taped television program.

29 January: American premiere of "Dr. Strangelove, or: How I Learned to Stop Worrying and Love the Bomb."

3 February: The Beatles arrive in America.

11 February: The fifth installment is completed.

25 February: NM is in the audience in Miami when Muhammad Ali defeats Sonny Liston for the heavyweight championship.

17 March: Beverly gives birth to Michael Burks Mailer, NM's first son, at about the same time that he completes the sixth installment.

20 April: The seventh installment is completed.

Late May: Warner Brothers buys an option on the film rights to *An American Dream*.

Early June: The eighth and final installment of the novel is completed. The Mailers go to Provincetown where NM will revise the *Esquire* version for book publication.

2 July: President Johnson signs the Civil Rights Act against discrimination.

Mid-July: NM break off work on the revision to the novel to cover the Republican Convention in San Francisco. His account, "In the Red Light," appears in the November *Esquire*.

7 August: The U.S. Congress passes the Tonkin Gulf Resolution authorizing the President to use military force in Vietnam.

September: The Free Speech movement begins at the University of California at Berkeley.

12 October: An advertisement for *An American Dream* in book form appears in *Publishers' Weekly* and gives a January 1965 publication date.

3 November: Johnson elected President.

20 December: Working on the Dial Press galleys, NM completes a second revision of the novel.

1965

Early January: NM testifies on behalf of William Burroughs's novel, *Naked Lunch,* at its Boston obscenity trial.

27 January: NM writes to his Japanese translator that Warner Brothers has purchased the film rights to the novel. It sells for $200,000.

21 February: Malcolm X is assassinated.

March 1965: U.S. troops arrive in force in Vietnam, escalating the War.

14 March: Tom Wolfe's negative review of the novel appears in *Book Week (Washington Post)*.

15 March: Official publication date of *An American Dream* by Dial Press.

19 March: "The Big Comeback of Norman Mailer," a positive review by John W. Aldridge, appears in *Life*. NM pays to reprint the heart of the review in the spring number of *Partisan Review* to "accompany" Elizabeth Hardwick's negative review.

27 March: The novel rises to number four on the bestseller list of the *Chicago Daily News*.

1 April: NM travels to Alaska for a four-day visit, speaking at the University of Alaska. He uses his impressions for his 1967 novel, *Why Are We in Vietnam?*

11 April: The novel rises to number eight on the bestseller list of the *New York Times Book Review.*

20 April: NM arrives in London to promote the British edition of *An American Dream*, published by Andre Deutsch on 26 April.

21 May: NM speaks out against the Vietnam War at the Berkeley campus of the University of California.

15 July: NM speaks at a Harvard teach-in against the Vietnam War.

Late July: NM travels to Puerto Rico for the Jose Torres-Tom McNeeley prizefight and meets with Muhammad Ali.

6 August: Voting Right Act of 1965, guaranteeing minority access to the polls, signed into law by President Johnson.

11 August: Race riots break out in Watts, Los Angeles.

Fall: NM contributes to a *Partisan Review* symposium, "On Vietnam."

24 September: Brock Brower's biographical article on NM appears in *Life.*

29 September: National Endowment for the Arts signed into law by President Johnson.

Late December: NM addresses the Modern Language Association meeting in Chicago on the American novel. His talk is published in the March 1966 issue of *Commentary.*

1966

March: The Dell paperback edition of *An American Dream* is published.

10 March: NM's second son, Stephen McLeod Mailer, is born to Beverly.

June: NM purchases a house at 565 Commercial Street in Provincetown.

August: The first stage version of NM's 1955 novel, *The Deer Park,* with Beverly Bentley as Lulu Meyers, is presented at Act IV, a Provincetown theater.

26 August: The film version of *An American Dream* premiers.

28 August: NM's review of Mark Lane's *Rush to Judgment,* an analysis of the Warren Commission Report on J.F.K.'s assassination, appears in *Book Week (Washington Post).*

29 August: Dial Press publishes *Cannibals and Christians,* NM's third volume of collected prose and poetry.

29 October: National Organization for Women established.

APPENDIX IV

An American Dream: Word Count Comparison, *Esquire* and Dial Press Versions

	Chapter Titles	*Esquire* Version	Dial Version
1	The Harbors of the Moon	11,708	11,394
2	A Messenger from the Casino	7,805	
	A Runner from the Gaming Room		7,066
3	A Messenger from the Maniac	14,406	14,540
4	Green Circles of Exhaustion	10,532	9,566
5	A Catenary of Manners	16,153	16,053
6	A Vision in the Desert	6,762	5,004
7	A Votive is Prepared	9,620	8,836
8	At the Lion and the Serpent	19,972	22,696
	Epilogue	1,811	
	Epilogue/The Harbors of the Moon Again		1,755
	TOTAL WORD COUNT	98,796	96,910

Index

K

L

M

The first edition of this book consists of 110 numbered copies, 10 of which are hors commerce copies, and 40 presentation copies. All 150 copies are signed by Norman Mailer and the editor.

This is copy _2nd editon, #52_